PUFFIN BOOKS

TALISMAN OF DEATH

The once-peaceful world of Orb is in terrible danger. Dark forces are at work to unleash the awesome might of the Evil One but their plans cannot be completed without the legendary Talisman of Death. It seems that all Orb is searching for the Talisman and yet YOU are the one who carries it. YOUR mission is to destroy the evil Talisman before the minions of Death can reach you. But beware! Time is running out. . .

Two dice, a pencil and an eraser are all you need to embark on this thrilling adventure of sword and sorcery, complete with its elaborate combat system and a score sheet to record your gains and losses.

Many dangers lie ahead and your success is by no means certain. Powerful adversaries are ranged against you and often your only choice is to kill or be killed!

The Fighting Fantasy Gamebooks

Steve Jackson and Ian Livingstone present:

TALISMAN OF DEATH

Jamie Thomson and Mark Smith
Illustrated by Bob Harvey

Puffin Books

Puffin Books, Penguin Books Ltd, Harmondsworth, Middlesex, England
Viking Penguin Inc., 40 West 23rd Street, New York, New York 10010, U.S.A.
Penguin Books Australia Ltd, Ringwood, Victoria, Australia
Penguin Books Canada Ltd, 2801 John Street, Markham, Ontario, Canada L3R 1B4
Penguin Books (N.Z.) Ltd, 182–190 Wairau Road, Auckland 10, New Zealand

First published 1984

Made and printed in Great Britain by
Cox & Wyman Ltd, Reading
Typeset in 11/13 pt Linotron Palatino by
Rowland Phototypesetting Ltd,
Bury St Edmunds, Suffolk

CONTENTS

HOW TO FIGHT THE CREATURES OF ORB

Before embarking on your adventure, you must first determine your own strengths and weaknesses. You have in your possession a sword, a backpack containing provisions (food and drink), and fire flares to combat the dark terrors of Orb. After weeks of intensive training, your sword-play is swift and deadly.

To discover the strength of your courage and the power of luck, you must use the dice to determine your initial STAMINA and LUCK scores. On pages **18–19** there is an *Adventure Sheet* which you may use to record the details of an adventure. On it you will find boxes for recording your SKILL and STAMINA and LUCK scores.

You are advised either to record your scores on the *Adventure Sheet* in pencil or to make photocopies of the page to use in future adventures.

Skill, Stamina and Luck

Roll one die. Add 6 to this number and enter this total in the SKILL box on the *Adventure Sheet*.

Roll both dice. Add 12 to the number rolled and enter this total in the STAMINA box.

Roll one die, add 6 to this number and enter this total in the LUCK box.

For reasons that will be explained below, SKILL, STAMINA and LUCK scores change constantly during an adventure. You must keep an accurate record of these scores and for this reason you are advised either to write small in the boxes or to keep an eraser handy. But never rub out your *Initial* scores. Although you may be awarded additional SKILL, STAMINA and LUCK points, these totals may never exceed your *Initial* scores.

Your SKILL score reflects your swordsmanship and general fighting expertise; the higher the better. Your STAMINA score reflects your general constitution, your will to survive, your determination and overall fitness; the higher your STAMINA score, the longer you will be able to survive. Your LUCK score indicates how naturally lucky a person you are. Luck – and magic – are facts of life in the fantasy kingdom you are about to explore.

Battles

You will often come across pages in the book which instruct you to fight a creature of some sort. An option to flee may be given, but if not – or if you choose to attack the creature anyway – you must resolve the battle as described below.

First record the creature's SKILL and STAMINA scores in the first vacant Monster Encounter Box on your *Adventure Sheet*. The scores for each creature are given in the book each time you have an encounter.

The sequence of combat is then:

1. Roll both dice once for the creature. Add its SKILL score. This total is the creature's Attack Strength.
2. Roll both dice once for yourself. Add the number rolled to your current SKILL score. This total is your Attack Strength.
3. If your Attack Strength is higher than that of the creature, you have wounded it. Proceed to step 4. If the creature's Attack Strength is higher than yours, it has wounded you. Proceed to step 5. If both Attack Strength totals are the same, you have avoided each other's blows – start the next Attack Round from step 1 above.
4. You have wounded the creature, so subtract 2 points from its STAMINA score. You may use your LUCK here to do additional damage (see over).

5. The creature has wounded you, so subtract 2 points from your own STAMINA score. Again you may use LUCK at this stage (see over).
6. Make the appropriate adjustments to either the creature's or your own STAMINA scores (and your LUCK score if you used LUCK – see over).
7. Begin the next Attack Round by returning to your current SKILL score and repeating steps 1–6. This sequence continues until the STAMINA score of either you or the creature you are fighting has been reduced to zero (death).

Escaping

On some pages you may be given the option of running away from a battle should things be going badly for you. However, if you do run away, the creature automatically gets in one wound on you (subtract 2 STAMINA points) as you flee. Such is the price of cowardice. Note that you may use LUCK on this wound in the normal way (see below). You may only *Escape* if that option is specifically given to you on the page.

Fighting More Than One Creature

Sometimes you will find yourself under attack from more than one person or creature. When this happens, each will have a separate attack on you in each Attack Round but you must choose which one you will fight. Attack your chosen target as in normal battle. Against the other, you must throw for your

Attack Strength in the normal way but, even if your Attack Strength is greater, you will not inflict a wound. Just count this as though you have parried an incoming blow. However, if your Attack Strength is lower, you will have been wounded in the normal way.

Luck

At various times during your adventure, either in battles or when you come across situations in which you could either be lucky or unlucky (details of these are given on the pages themselves), you may call on your LUCK to make the outcome more favourable. But beware! Using LUCK is a risky business and if you are *unlucky*, the results could be disastrous.

The procedure for using your LUCK is as follows: roll two dice. If the number rolled is equal to or less than your current LUCK score, you have been lucky and the result will go in your favour. If the number rolled is higher than your current LUCK score, you have been unlucky and you will be penalized.

This procedure is known as *Testing your Luck*. Each time you *Test your Luck*, you must subtract one point from your current LUCK score. Thus you will soon realize that the more you rely on your LUCK, the more risky this will become.

Using Luck in Battles

On certain pages of the book you will be told to *Test your Luck* and will be told the consequences of your being lucky or unlucky. However, in battles, you always have the option of using your LUCK either to inflict a more serious wound on a creature you have just wounded, or to minimize the effects of a wound the creature has just inflicted on you.

If you have just wounded the creature, you may *Test your Luck* as described above. If you are Lucky, you have inflicted a severe wound and may subtract an *extra* 2 points from the creature's STAMINA score. However, if you are Unlucky, the wound was a mere graze and you must restore 1 point to the creature's STAMINA (i.e. instead of scoring the normal 2 points of damage, you have now scored only 1).

If the creature has just wounded you, you may *Test your Luck* to try to minimize the wound. If you are Lucky, you have managed to avoid the full damage of the blow. Restore 1 point of STAMINA (i.e. instead of doing 2 points of damage it has one only 1). If you are Unlucky, you have taken a more serious blow. Subtract 1 extra STAMINA point.

Remember that you must subtract 1 point from your own LUCK score each time you *Test your Luck*.

Restoring Skill, Stamina and Luck

Skill

Your SKILL score will not change much during your adventure. Occasionally, a page may give instructions to increase or decrease your SKILL score. A Magic Weapon may increase your SKILL, but remember that only one weapon can be used at a time! You cannot claim 2 SKILL bonuses for carrying two Magic Swords. Your SKILL score can never exceed its *Initial* value. Drinking the Potion of Skill (see later) will restore your SKILL to its *Initial* level at any time.

Stamina and Provisions

Your STAMINA score will change a lot during your adventure as you fight monsters and undertake arduous tasks. As you near your goal, your STAMINA level may be dangerously low and battles may be particularly risky, so be careful!

Your backpack contains enough Provisions for ten meals. You may rest and eat at any time except when engaged in a Battle. Eating a meal restores 4 STAMINA points. When you eat a meal, add 4 points to your STAMINA score and deduct 1 point from your Provisions. A separate Provisions Remaining box is provided on the *Adventure Sheet* for recording details of Provisions. Remember that you have a long way to go, so use your Provisions wisely!

Remember also that your STAMINA score may never exceed its *Initial* value. Drinking the Potion of Strength (see later) will restore your STAMINA to its *Initial* level at any time.

Luck

Additions to your LUCK score are awarded through the adventure when you have been particularly lucky. Details are given on the pages of the book. Remember that, as with SKILL and STAMINA, your LUCK score may never exceed its *Initial* value. Drinking the Potion of Fortune (see later) will restore your LUCK to its *Initial* level at any time, and increase your *Initial* LUCK by 1 point.

EQUIPMENT AND POTIONS

You will start your adventure with a bare minimum of equipment, but you may find or buy other items during your travels. You are armed with a sword and are dressed in leather armour. You have a backpack to hold your Provisions and any treasures you may come across.

In addition, you may take one bottle of a magic potion which will aid you on your quest. You may choose to take a bottle of any of the following:

A Potion of Skill – restores SKILL points
A Potion of Strength – restores STAMINA points
A Potion of Fortune – restores LUCK points and adds 1 to *Initial* LUCK

These potions may be taken at any time during your adventure (except when engaged in a Battle). Taking a measure of potion will restore SKILL, STAMINA or LUCK scores to their *Initial* level (and the Potion of Fortune will add 1 point to your *Initial* LUCK score before LUCK is restored).

Each bottle of potion contains enough for *one* measure, i.e. the characteristic may be restored once during an adventure. Make a note on your *Adventure Sheet* when you have used up a potion.

Remember also that you may only choose *one* of the three potions to take on your trip, so choose wisely!

To explore the network of caves and tunnels and to combat the terrors of the night, you are also equipped with five torches. To light them you have a flint and tinder – guard them with your life!

HINTS ON PLAY

There is one true way through the mysterious world of Orb and it will take you several attempts to find it. Make notes and draw a map as you explore – this map will be invaluable in future adventures and enable you to progress rapidly through to unexplored sections.

Not all areas contain treasure; some merely contain traps and creatures which you will no doubt fall foul of. You may make wrong turnings during your quest and while you may indeed progress through to your ultimate destination, it is by no means certain that you will find what you are searching for.

It will be realized that entries make no sense if read in numerical order. It is essential that you read only the entries you are instructed to read. Reading other entries will only cause confusion and may lessen the excitement during play.

The one true way involves a minimum of risk and any player, no matter how weak on initial dice rolls, should be able to get through fairly easily.

May the luck of the gods go with you on the adventure ahead!

ADVENTURE SHEET

SKILL	STAMINA	LUCK
Initial Skill= 9	Initial Stamina= 18	Initial Luck= 18

EQUIPMENT LIST

Sword, leather
armor, rucksack,
Sap of the
Willow,

GOLD

JEWELS

POTIONS

Strength 1

PROVISIONS REMAINING

Food 10

MONSTER ENCOUNTER BOXES

Skill= *Stamina=* 16	*Skill=* *Stamina=*	*Skill=* *Stamina=*
Skill= *Stamina=*	*Skill=* *Stamina=*	*Skill=* *Stamina=*
Skill= *Stamina=*	*Skill=* *Stamina=*	*Skill=* *Stamina=*
Skill= *Stamina=*	*Skill=* *Stamina=*	*Skill=* *Stamina=*

BACKGROUND

You are regaining consciousness. Your eyes flutter open to the sound of a songbird, trilling joyously. You are lying on a couch of green velvet, set on the topmost turret of a great white castle hanging in the clouds. Rising to your feet you look around. The songbird, whose sleek feathers are a warm burnished gold, is perched on the battlements, resplendent against the ocean-blue canopy of a sky in which there is no sun.

You are clad in strange, outlandish clothes, breeches of dark-green leather and a thickly quilled leather jerkin. On your feet are russet-red calfskin boots, supple and comfortable, into which the breeches are tucked at mid-calf. A heavy sword is belted at your side and, with a shock, you realize that somehow you know how to use it skilfully and with deadly force. As the songbird trills you try, in vain, to recall memories of Earth but everything is hazy and distant. You have been taken from the world you know and trained in the art of swordplay. You cannot remember even who trained you or why, but the hilt of the sword fits your hand snugly. Drawing it, you lunge and parry, marvelling at how the sword cuts through the air faster than the eye can follow.

The songbird seems unperturbed by your fine

display of swordsmanship, but you are surprised when it cocks its head and speaks to you, its voice fluting merrily.

'Welcome, Champion of Fate. Do not be dismayed, you are not yet in danger.'

'Where am I?' you ask, feeling as if you are in a dream.

'Far, far from your home, I fear to say. This is the world of Orb and you are in the Garden of the Gods.'

'What is Orb?' you demand.

'You will find it most strange and full of wonder, for it is very different from Earth. Men must share it not just with talking creatures such as I but with weird and fell monsters, giants, dragons and demons. There are warlocks and sorcerers, too, great wielders of magic, in the cities. But do not fear, you have been chosen to be our champion, for you are more likely to succeed than any other on Earth. Now I must complete my task. Come, my masters bid you join them in the chamber below. Please follow me.'

With that the golden songbird flutters away down a spiral staircase. Shaking your head in confusion you descend the stone steps into a large circular room where two beings turn towards you. 'Welcome,' says one, a pale female figure enfolded in a swirling robe of many colours above which you can only see a perfectly smooth and hairless head. The robe shimmers, its colours shifting as she steps towards you, catching your mind before you realize what is happening. Looking into her face, you see an image of yourself, fighting for your life inside a huge temple. Then the image shifts and you see yourself leaving a walled city, hastening alone across a desolate moor, only to find yourself deep in a jungle, surrounded by devils with blue skins. Your nape bristles as you realize that she is revealing glimpses of your destiny. It is only when they are over that you notice she has no eyes in her smooth pale face.

The other figure changes even as you look at him. At one moment he is an ancient white-haired man, heavy with knowledge, at another an infant, wise beyond his years. The metamorphosis through youth to age takes but a few instants, yet flows so smoothly you cannot see the features change. His voice is soft and ageless. 'We have summoned you here to the world of Orb because we wish to prevent a fatal upset in the balance of nature. The cosmic scales have been tipped too far and you must play a part in righting them. It is not for us in the Garden of the Gods to set things right. We cannot fight him who would bring chaos to Orb. Rather we use men as our tools. I shall not say whether you will succeed.'

The floor of the room upon which you are standing is the most realistic and detailed map imaginable. You can even see small figures tilling the fields and walking the streets of an entire world; a world of pinnacled castles; knights on horseback, their men-at-arms bearing banners which stream in the wind;

and strange high-walled cities with towers and spires, concealing the dives of assassins and thieves amongst the splendour. The eyeless immortal steps forward, her robe now the colour of the deep sea, and caresses your cheek.

'We are sending you down to the surface of Orb. If you fall into the clutches of Death we cannot aid you. Do not fail us!'

'Fail in what?' you begin to ask. But just then, to your horror, you find yourself being drawn inexorably towards a black crack in the map. The realization that your destiny is being tampered with angers you, and you resolve to find a way back to Earth and your home at any cost. As the world of Orb rises up to engulf you, the awesomeness of what is happening overwhelms you and you lose consciousness.

NOW TURN OVER

1

When awareness returns you look around. You are standing in a huge vaulted chamber, deep underground. In the chill air you wonder what terrible fate may be in store for you. You are utterly alone, without a friend in the world, and you have no idea what fiendish horrors may exist here, so far from home. There are no windows in the chamber, nor natural light, only the ruddy glow of flaming torches that are fixed to pillars soaring beyond sight. The walls are running with damp, the air musty and heavy with age. There are two archways at the back of the cavern. Before you can investigate further, the torchlight flickers, and a cool gust chills you to the marrow; something in the unseen darkness is causing the air to move. A light flashes briefly ahead and an infernal howling echoes across the vast vault. No living thing could possibly have made that dreadful sound, you think to yourself, but then you remember that you know nothing of the dreadful denizens of Orb. You hear the sound of running footsteps approaching rapidly; you cannot yet see who or what is coming. Will you run through the nearest archway (turn to **17**), or hold your ground and draw your sword (turn to **30**)?

2

There is an uneasy silence in the ale cellar. Tyutchev looks across at you and says, 'I don't like your face.' Cassandra nods agreement. If you retort, 'At least, unlike you, I am wholesome to look upon,' turn to **294**. If you meekly reply, 'I'm sorry, I was born that way,' and leave the ale cellar, turn to **305**.

3

You ask the barman for a mug of ale. While he pours you your drink, your eyes adjust to the gloom and you survey his customers. You have never seen a more disreputable bunch of villainous-looking cut-throats. The barman says, 'That will be a piece of gold.' You hand over the money. As you replace your money-pouch a dozen pairs of eyes watch closely. The only one who doesn't watch is a stooped old man, cleaning slops off an empty table. Will you:

Talk to the barman?	Turn to **88**
Walk over to the old man?	Turn to **19**
Approach six surly-looking men, who look like thieves?	Turn to **280**

4

The Pteranodon, mortally wounded, crashes into the undergrowth. You struggle on; the heat is oppressive and you are plagued by flies, which circle between the tall straight conifers. Creepers trail from the overhanging branches and great ferns cover the ground. The air is alive with strange noises, and huge dragonflies, vibrantly coloured, hum from flower to giant flower. Suddenly, with a report like a rifle, a tree-trunk snaps. The ground shakes as a huge prehistoric monster charges at you. Three long horns project from the bony carapace which protects its neck. You must fight . . .

TRICERATOPS   SKILL 8   STAMINA 30

After three rounds of combat you hear shrill cries of alarm as another great beast thunders towards you. *Test your Luck*. If you are Lucky, turn to **40**. If you are Unlucky, turn to **25**.

5

You charge at the Shieldmaiden. She coolly takes aim and unleashes a crossbow bolt. It slams into the shoulder of your sword-arm, crippling it with a searing pain. Lose 1 SKILL point and 2 STAMINA points. As you fall, the Shieldmaiden places her sword at your throat. 'Don't make a move if you wish to live,' she says. Turn to **75**.

The servant says, 'Ah yes, you are expected. Please come in.' You follow him into the parlour. The dining-table is laid for three. Apothecus rises to greet you and introduces you to his friend, Diodorus, a Sage who is an expert on travel between the planes of existence. He tells you that there are portals or gates, allowing travel between Orb and other worlds. He suspects that you may have been brought from Earth to Orb by means of such a portal. 'When you recover the Talisman,' he says, 'you must leave Greyguilds and walk south-east until you come to the Great Plateau. Mount Starreach, the tallest mountain on the plateau, has, at its summit, one of these portals, through which you must pass if you wish to return to Earth.'

'And now to more immediate matters,' says Apothecus. 'You can leave the city by the postern gate in the cemetery. If you get into serious trouble you may be able to call on the All-Mother for aid. To do so cry, "All-Mother, nature herself, preserve me."' He makes you repeat the words and you commit them to memory; note them on your Adventure Sheet. He explains that the All-Mother is the Fountain of all Life, the opposite of Death. She may be prepared to help you, but only once, at the time of your greatest need. 'However, remember this: no deity can intervene in another's temple.' You thank them both and turn in early after the sumptuous meal of peacock basted in Spirits of Ra, and other exotic dishes. You wake up refreshed –

gain 4 STAMINA points. You bid Apothecus fare-well, thanking him for all his help and hoping that you won't let him down. You set out to find the Thieves' Guild. Turn to 64.

7

You light a torch and enter the cavern, which stretches away into blackness. You scramble across the cavern floor until you see a small smooth-walled tunnel branching off from the main tunnel. The strong smell of sulphur seems to pervade both. Will you walk down the wide and rocky main tunnel (turn to 378), or investigate the narrow tunnel (turn to 48)?

8

You put several miles between yourself and Greyguilds and sleep the night in a hayrick. You awake refreshed. Gain 2 STAMINA points. Which direction will you take towards the plateau? You could take the direct route, south-east, across rough moorland; continue along the old trade road, due south for a while and then strike east; or head east across the heath to the hills before turning south.

South-east   Turn to **287**
South, then east   Turn to **300**
East, then south   Turn to **313**

9

You lie still, enfolded in the Roc's talons, as it wings its ponderous way to the purple mountains. Soon you are spiralling up the mountainside to the Roc's eyrie. The Roc lets you fall on to the feather-soft nest and prepares to dismember you before feeding you to its two enormous chicks. You must fight the Roc. Each time you make a successful attack, roll one die. If you throw a 1 turn to **55**.

ROC   SKILL 10   STAMINA 16

If you win, turn to **84**.

10

You attack the Dragon! 'I shall rend you limb from limb,' it roars. The great claws swipe at you as it tries to crush your head in its enormous jaws.

RED DRAGON   SKILL 12   STAMINA 20

If you reduce the Dragon's STAMINA to 5 or less, turn to **29**.

You stop at the bar and are about to ask the barman what there is to drink, when you hear yourself saying, 'You fat pig, pour me a drink before the sight of your squalid pus-ridden face makes me vomit.' The barman stiffens, astonished and incensed. He gives a strangled cry of rage, grabs his club and hurdles the bar. You step back, drawing your sword. Your eyes have adjusted to the gloom and you notice that some of his customers are rising to their feet. They are the most disreputable bunch of villainous-looking cut-throats you have ever seen; one has a scar running from his ear to his chin. You must fight the barman and one other.

	SKILL	STAMINA
BARMAN	7	8
First CUT-THROAT	8	9

If you reduce the barman's STAMINA to 4 or less he scuttles back behind the bar. If you can then reduce the First Cut-throat's STAMINA to 5 or less, *Test your Luck*. If you are Lucky, turn to **200**. If you are Unlucky, turn to **181**.

12

Your first blow is fatal. Blood spurts from a gaping wound and the old man falls to the ground. You step back as he turns once more into his normal form, that of a huge Red Dragon. The Guardian Dragon of the portals is dead. You step towards the silver shimmering portal. Turn to **400**.

13

A woman wearing chainmail and carrying a loaded crossbow bursts into the torchlight ahead of you. Seeing you, she immediately points the bow in your direction. Three men, panting heavily, appear behind her. The first, a tall and handsome man, is dressed in shining silver armour and the blade of his two-handed sword glows with a faint white radiance. The next is dressed in a flowing robe of cloth of gold and wears a smiling golden mask. He carries an ivory staff. The last is a thick-set man with a white surcoat over chainmail. A red cross adorns his breast and a spiked mace hangs at his side. They stop. Once again you hear a wailing, louder than before. 'They are almost upon us,' cries the man with the glittering sword. The Shieldmaiden calls to you, 'Who are you and what are you doing here in the Rift, the spawning place of all evil?' Will you:

Say you have come from another world?	Turn to **247**
Say that you are on a quest against evil?	Turn to **60**
Try to play for time?	Turn to **75**
Attack the Shieldmaiden?	Turn to **5**

14

You camp for the night, but some large black flies, which had just seemed a nuisance, are now objects of fear, since their eggs have hatched and you are food for their larvae. You get no rest, and don't regain any STAMINA as a result. At dawn you plunge into an algae-covered pool and the larvae fall from you. Feeling better you begin the march towards the foothills of Mount Star-reach. Soon you are climbing the mountain itself, grasping at the stunted bushes which grow on its slopes. You notice that the air is becoming thinner, and you are short of breath when you reach a wide cave mouth, which smells faintly of sulphur. Intrigued, you decide to enter the cave. Turn to **7**.

15

The taproom of the inn is empty. You ask for a hot meal and a room for the night. The innkeeper tells you that this will cost you three pieces of gold, but says that he is short-handed and that if you will do the washing-up he will let you stay for nothing. The choice is yours. You have a delicious meal of roast hippogriff in cream sauce. After your meal you sleep like a log and wake up feeling refreshed. Gain 4 STAMINA points. You set out in search of the Thieves' Guild. Turn to **64**.

16

The doors open easily. It seems the magic has faded now that Hawkana is truly dead. The thieves have been spying on you through the keyhole. Scarface says, 'The door was locked and we couldn't get in.' He leads the way back up to the skylight. If you still have Hawkana's ring, you feel it grow cold and see that it has tarnished to a dull grey metal. Its magic only works within the Inner Sanctum. Suddenly, the alarm bell tolls loudly. As you reach the top landing, a group of warrior-women appears on the stairs behind you in hot pursuit. You all run for the rope hanging from the skylight. As you reach it, you sense a movement at your side and dodge the murderous thrust of Bloodheart's dagger just in time. Before he can strike again, the warrior-women let loose a volley of crossbow bolts. Bloodheart's body is peppered with quarrels, shielding you as you climb the rope. Leaving the stricken Bloodheart to his fate, the remaining thieves jump agilely from the temple roof to the roof of a nearby house. You will have to jump, too. Roll two dice. If the total is less than or equal to your SKILL score, turn to **163**. If it is greater than your SKILL score, turn to **56**.

17

As you dash towards the forbidding blackness of the archway, you hear a click followed by a rumbling sound ahead. The floor beneath your feet begins to tremble. Do you want to hurl yourself through the archway, into the darkness (turn to **41**), or stop your headlong flight (turn to **21**)?

18

The Roc appears not to notice your futile attack and you are swept up as the Roc begins to climb towards the purple mountains. You are too high to risk struggling. Turn to **9**.

19

The toothless old man mutters at you. He tells you that this ale cellar is a dangerous place. Having given his warning, he shuffles fearfully away. Will you go back to the bar (turn to **88**), or go over to the table where six surly-looking men are sitting (turn to **280**)?

20

At last the steep cliffs surrounding the plateau tower above you. Steps have been cut into the face of the reddish rock, which you begin to climb. By midday your legs ache abominably and you are glad to reach a ledge where you are welcomed by a cool fine spray rising from a waterfall. It cascades down the side of the plateau, casting small rainbows in the sun, and the thunderous roar is almost deafening. Will you climb on up the steps (turn to **328**), or examine the waterfall (turn to **33**)?

21

You stop just in time – a slab of smooth rock slams down from above with a crash that reverberates around the cavern. It blocks the arch completely. The other one is similarly sealed. Realizing that you have no choice, you turn to face the oncoming footsteps and draw your sword. Turn to **13**.

22

You walk down the winding tunnel for some time. It bends gently to the left and downwards and eventually opens out into the large cavern. The dragon lies before you, but this time you are behind it. A few of its old scales lie littered around it. Will you:

Thrust your spear, if you have one, into its scaly back?	Turn to **285**
Try to grab some scales?	Turn to **269**
Try to grab some of the treasure?	Turn to **38**
Leave the cavern?	Turn to **369**

23

She strikes you down, before helping you to your feet. You walk together into the Valley of Death, where your spirit will wander alone until the end of time.

24

You go down the steps and emerge into a long low cellar, set with tables and stools. The only light part is the bar, behind which stands the bulky proprietor of the inn. Turn to **3**.

25

As you step back to lunge again at the wild monster, you see a huge carnivore appear behind it. This must be what the Triceratops was running from. Now it shuffles round to face the TYRANNO-SAURUS, which is as tall as a house, with massive jaws. A gargantuan battle ensues. Finally the torn and bleeding Triceratops is knocked on to its side. The end is swift, as the foot-long incisors of the Tyrannosaurus bury themselves in the throat of the fallen monster. The victorious creature swivels its glassy eye to face you and raises its head. Seeing new prey it leaps towards you to snap you up. You must fight.

TYRANNOSAURUS   SKILL 11   STAMINA 18

If you win turn to **14**.

26

With a mighty blow, your sword cuts through one of the Willow's branches and some sap from the tree falls on to your arm. The Willow gives a low moan, stops attacking and pulls its branches back from you. Will you plunge your arm into the pool (turn to **161**), or beat a hasty retreat (turn to **39**)?

27

The Roc misses you and soars up into the sky. Luckily, its attention is distracted by larger prey. The Roc swoops again, with a roar of wind, and carries off a wild horse. Grateful for your luck you hasten on towards the plateau. Turn to **20**.

28

You turn down Carriage Street and see the sign of an inn, the Silver Trinket. It is next to a large stable and work-house. It seems a much more pleasant place than the Red Dragon Inn and, as it is growing late, you decide to go in. Turn to **15**.

29

Suddenly, your weapon is flailing at air. The Dragon has changed into an old man, with long white hair, wearing a white robe. 'Spare me, I beg you,' he implores, in a thin reedy voice. 'At last you have lifted the curse that was upon me. Only a strong warrior like yourself could have done it. When I came through the portal, many centuries ago, I was doomed to stay in the form of a dragon until I was beaten in combat. Now that I am myself again I can return to my world. Will you step through the portal with me?' Will you agree and walk with him into the silver shimmering portal (turn to **77**), or attack him (turn to **12**)?

30

The footsteps are coming closer; suddenly, a sound like a clap of thunder reverberates around the chamber. You look round and see that both the archways have been sealed by huge stone blocks. You are trapped. Turn to **13**.

31

The doors are still magically sealed shut. You cannot force them open. You turn to see that Hawkana has risen to her feet and taken up her sword again. Her eyes are filled with malice. 'You cannot kill me. This time I will carve out your spleen.' She is slower than before but you must fight her again.

HAWKANA   SKILL 9   STAMINA 6

If you win, turn to 54.

32

The brass tiger has a mischievous grin. You hang it round your neck, hoping it will bring luck or protection. Turn to 156.

33

You approach the waterfall and within moments are soaked through. Looking closer, you see a dry space behind it, under the jutting cliff-face. When you jump through, a cave entrance is revealed. Will you enter the cave (turn to **42**), or leave and continue up the steps (turn to **328**)?

34

Deftly you dodge the flailing claw and move in to the attack. Do you have a spear? If you do, turn to **51**. If not, turn to **10**.

35

You make some unintelligible signs and grunts, pointing to your mouth and ears. For a moment some of them think that you are casting a spell and draw their swords, but soon you hear one of them saying, 'A deaf warrior – well, there's a turn-up for the scrolls!' The Captain motions you to mount behind one of the younger women, Elvira, who does not seem pleased at having to share her horse with you. You ride for some time and after a while the women resume their normal conversation. You realize they are members of the Watch, or law-enforcers from Greyguilds-on-the-Moor. You also realize that there is rivalry between them and the Priestesses of the All-Mother in that city. It appears that the leniency of the Priestesses has annoyed them. Turn to **197**.

36

You struggle to overcome the drowsiness and the spell is broken. Looking up you can see two large green eyes staring at you from the trunk of the willow. Before you can step back you are attacked by the branches of the enraged tree. You must fight the WILLOW WEIRD.

WILLOW WEIRD   SKILL 8   STAMINA 20

If you make four successful attacks, turn to **26**.

37

The ROC's eyesight is as sharp as any eagle's. You are plucked from the ground like a harvest-mouse. The Roc begins to climb towards the purple mountains and away from the plateau. You are soon too high to risk struggling. Turn to **9**.

38

You make a grab for a jewel-encrusted helmet but trip, in your haste, over a golden chest full of black pearls. The Dragon hears you, turns and breathes on you as you are struggling to your feet. Rolling jets of flame consume you and you are charred to a cinder. Turn to **43**.

39

You wend your way along the bank of the river that runs west from the spring and leave the ferns behind. The terrain has become a little more open now. Looking back, your heart quickens as you catch sight of one of the Dark Elves sniffing at your trail. He moves with a lithe swiftness which would seem graceful, if it wasn't for his spiked black armour, and deadly expression. While you are watching, he stands up and points in your direction; they are not far behind. You must decide quickly. Will you:

Run along the river bank?	Turn to **359**
Plunge into the river and run along for some distance before scrambling up the bank?	Turn to **253**
Hide in a clump of bushes?	Turn to **307**

40

As you step back to lunge again at the wild monster you see a huge carnivore appear behind it. This must be what the Triceratops was running from. Now it shuffles round to face the TYRANNO-SAURUS and a gargantuan battle ensues. Finally, the torn and bleeding Triceratops thrusts forward, goring the Tyrannosaurus, which then crashes to the ground, fatally wounded. The Triceratops limps away and, breathing a sigh of relief, you move on towards the mountain. Turn to **14**.

41

Before you can charge through the archway a slab of smooth rock slams down from above, with a sound like a clap of thunder that reverberates around the cavern. It blocks the archway completely. Unfortunately you cannot stop in mid-leap; you crash sickeningly into the stone with bone-jarring force. Lose 2 STAMINA points. Feeling somewhat groggy, you pick yourself up and realize that the other archway is similarly sealed. Seeing you have no option you turn to face the oncoming footsteps and draw your sword. Turn to **13**.

42

You manage to light a damp torch, which reveals a door at the back of the cave. The door is made of a black wood, inlaid with alabaster. A raised frieze in the centre panel depicts a red dragon, a great flame shooting from its jaws, and an ivory spear. The door creaks as you open it gingerly. You step into a passage. The musty air reeks of decay. You come to a place where four tunnels cross. Will you:

Advance down the tunnel ahead?	Turn to **71**
Take the left-hand tunnel?	Turn to **53**
Take the right-hand tunnel?	Turn to **80**

43

Your spirit floats gently towards the Valley of Death. The featureless, wind-blasted plain stretches away endlessly, beyond the horizon. The souls of the dead wander there aimlessly, in solitude. Just as you approach the edge of the valley, an ethereal wind gets up and your soul is wafted away. Soon you feel yourself in the presence of the two who summoned you to this fantastic world of magic. The eyeless being in robes of shifting hues says, 'All is not yet lost.' You understand the words without hearing them. 'If your spirit is willing we will reunite it with your body and turn back the wheels of time.' The other being offers you a choice: 'If you wish it, I will send you back in time. You will be leaving Greyguilds.' Do you wish to go back in time to attempt the quest again? If you do, the being lays a hand on your shoulder. They disappear. You are alive again. You have 15 STAMINA points and all of the equipment you carried with you when you died, apart from the following, if you had picked them up: the Gum of an Amber Pine, the Feather of a Roc, the Spear, or the Scales of a Dragon. Cross these off your Adventure Sheet. You find yourself outside the city of Greyguilds. Turn to **8**.

44

Hawkana collapses to the floor, lifeless. You walk to the altar and take the Talisman of Death. It is cold and heavy. At last you have regained it. Gain 1 LUCK point. You look back at Hawkana and your scalp crawls. Her wounds are healing. Even as you watch she tries to raise herself from the pool of blood in which she lies. Will you go back to Hawkana (turn to 54), or run to the double doors (turn to 31)?

45

You fight Harg. Your blows cause black blood to flow, but the wounds close up as fast as you can inflict them. Harg's hammer catches you on the shoulder – lose 2 STAMINA points. At this Thaum snaps his fingers and Harg, an illusion after all, disappears. Turn to 171.

46

You raise the Talisman above your head. It glows as you shout: 'Begone! Trouble me no more!' Enthralled, they strain towards it, but your words have an immediate effect. One of them cries, 'Others will take it from you and we Faceless Ones will return as lords under the reign of our God, Death.' His words fade as they are swallowed by the darkness. The Talisman feels lighter and its glow has dimmed. You sleep deeply, and gain 2 STAMINA points. The next day you set off again, feeling more hopeful now that you have banished the minions of Death. The plateau looms before you. Turn to **20**.

47

The angry young man turns to you, a puzzled expression on his face. He thanks you and says, 'I don't know why we are quarrelling really.' He takes the charm from you and you walk on. Fortune will smile on you for being so honest (gain 1 LUCK point). Soon afterwards you hear the fight breaking out again. 'You're always making trouble,' shouts the other young man. You leave them to it. Turn to **156**.

48

You walk down the winding tunnel for some time, until it opens out into a large cavern. In front of you is the ridged back of an immense Dragon. It is about eighteen metres long and is covered in thick red scales. Its long tail is curled round a vast hoard of treasure – gems, gold, goblets and vases – which lies higgledy-piggledy beneath its bulk. A few of its old scales are littered around it. Will you:

Thrust your spear, if you have one, into its scaly back?	Turn to 285
Try to grab some of its scales?	Turn to 269
Try to grab some of the Dragon's treasure?	Turn to 38
Leave the cavern?	Turn to 369

49

You walk through the front door, which is glistening with frost. A trail of frost leads from the door to a large pentacle chalked on the floor. Sand is strewn where the frost crosses the edge of the pentacle. On a table lie various strange pieces of equipment. On the floor next to it lies an Amulet, made from the tip of a Unicorn's Horn, with strange runes engraved on it. You may take it if you wish. There appears to be nothing else of any use to you, so you leave. Turn to 28.

50

Hawkana draws her sword and advances on you, snarling with tigerish ferocity. You must fight the High Priestess.

HAWKANA   SKILL 12   STAMINA 14

If you win, go to **44**.

51

You attack the dragon. 'I shall rend you limb from limb,' it roars. The great claws swipe at you as it tries to crush your head in its enormous jaws. You dodge to one side as it leaps at you and thrust your spear at its soft underbelly.

RED DRAGON   SKILL 12   STAMINA 20

Each time you make a successful attack deduct 5 STAMINA points from the Dragon's total, as the magical spear seems to bite deep into its flesh. If you reduce the Dragon's STAMINA to 5 or less, turn to **29**.

Cross one of your Provisions off your Adventure Sheet. Crouching on one knee, you toss the dried meat to the wolf, speaking in soothing tones as you do so. The wolf accepts your gift. Then a green-robed figure steps into the clearing. He has an oak staff in one hand and a silver sickle in the other. A crown of mistletoe rests on his head. He smiles at you and says, 'My name is Wodeman. I am the Guardian Druid of this Sacred Grove. My friend, Snowmane, thanks you for the gift of food. Such gentle generosity deserves reward. The Blessing of the Druids will go with you. May fortune smile on you.' You gain 1 LUCK point for the Druid's Blessing. 'You look weary,' he says. 'Here, have this.' He takes a golden apple from his robes and hands it to you. Note it down on your Adventure Sheet – such apples are wonderfully refreshing and will restore up to 4 STAMINA points when you eat one. You thank him, and knowing you must continue on your quest, reluctantly leave the idyllic peace of the Sacred Grove. Turn to **159**.

53

You take the left-hand tunnel, which soon turns to the right, and leads into a bare stone room with a small rectangular pillar in the middle. The tunnel continues on the other side of the room. Will you:

Examine the pillar?	Turn to **136**
Go straight through to the tunnel opposite?	Turn to **89**
Return to where the tunnels crossed and choose again?	Turn to **42**

54

You notice that a ring on Hawkana's finger is glowing with a green light as her wounds close up. Quickly you take it off before she comes fully back to life. You place it on your own finger. It is a Ring of Regeneration; regain 6 STAMINA points. Will you now try to leave through the double doors (turn to **16**), or search the Inner Sanctum (turn to **137**)?

55

You manage to drive your sword into one of the Roc's huge eyes. It screeches in pain and flies away from the eyrie. You seize your chance to escape. Turn to **84**.

56

You fly through the air, but not far enough. You slam into the side of the building with bone-shattering force and plummet to the street below. Luck has not deserted you completely, for you land in a stinking pile of refuse, which breaks your fall a little. Lose 3 STAMINA points. If you are still alive, you drag yourself off down an alleyway which leads towards the safe house. Near the safe house you pause to rest before leaving the city. Turn to **235**.

57

You take a side-street which leads towards the Street of Seven Sins and are almost pushed aside by a couple of students in blue togas. They are quarrelling and begin fighting in front of you. It seems one of them disagrees violently with something the other has said. As they tussle, you notice that the angry young man has dropped a small brass tiger charm. Will you:

Interrupt the quarrel and give the charm back?	Turn to **47**
Ignore them and go on your way?	Turn to **156**
Pick up the charm?	Turn to **32**

58

You hurl yourself at the rolling shield and just manage to grasp its rim. You cover yourself with it as you lie there. The dragon breathes on you again and one of your legs, left unshielded, is badly burned. Lose 4 STAMINA points. If you are still alive, you get up and attack once more. If you have a spear, turn to **51**. If you have not, turn to **10**.

59

After that display of power, you hurriedly use your Scroll of Agonizing Doom. Hawkana draws her sword and advances on you, snarling with tigerish ferocity. But the spell works and a crackling electric-blue aura surrounds her. She throws back her head and howls with agony. She is very badly hurt and staggers, but then exerts her will and recovers. You must fight the High Priestess.

HAWKANA   SKILL 12   STAMINA 6

If you win, turn to **44**.

60

'Alone?' asks the Shieldmaiden in disbelief. The man in gold turns to the Priest. 'Is it true?' he asks. Knowing your story to be a lie you wait anxiously while the Priest casts a spell. 'It is a lie,' says the Priest. The Shieldmaiden turns to you accusingly. 'Why are you lying to us? I ask you again, who are you and what are you doing here?' Will you tell them the truth (turn to **70**), or ask them what business it is of theirs (turn to **75**)?

61

You have banished the Ice Demon to the plane from which it came, through defeating it in combat. The shards of broken glass crunch underfoot. Will you enter the house it came from (turn to **49**), or continue down Cobbler's Walk (turn to **28**)?

62

With a clatter of armour the Death-knight folds at the knees and vanishes. A vision of the Paladin appears. 'Well done. You are a valiant warrior, worthy of the quest. Here, take my Holy Sword: it will aid you, for I no longer can.' He hands you his glittering sword and the vision fades. The sword feels real enough and its glow lights up the stable. Your wounds are healed magically as you touch it (regain up to 6 STAMINA points) – a gift from the Paladin. You may add 1 to your SKILL when using the Holy Sword. Turn to **121**.

63

You run as fast you can along the rocky ground. Your lungs are burning with the effort. As you approach the hills, you look back and see that both groups are now roughly the same distance behind you. The Elves coming from the north are in a tight pack, while the Orcs to the south are beginning to string out. Will you:

Head north to meet the Elves?	Turn to **214**
Climb a hill to the south, to face the Orcs?	Turn to **282**
Run on?	Turn to **227**

64

As you set off, you see a small group of people clustered around a man wearing a flowing grey cloak and one dangling gold ear-ring. He is making huge bunches of flowers appear and disappear to cries of delight and amusement from the crowd. Will you:

Try to find a way into the Thieves'
Guild?   Turn to **83**

Try to regain the Talisman on your
own?   Turn to **383**

Stay and watch the magic?   Turn to **106**

65

Eventually, the hills give way to a desolate grey
moor stretching out to the west. After half an hour
or so, you see a cloud of dust ahead. You can soon
make out a group of twenty horsemen. They wheel
their steeds towards you and the drumming of
hoofs carries to you over the breeze. As they get
nearer, you can see that this is a band of warrior-
women, clad in chainmail and studded leather
armour. Their faces look grim and unwelcoming as
they wheel around you, forming a closed circle.
Their Captain spurs her horse forward and tersely
demands what you are doing out here, alone on the
edge of the moor. Will you:

Tell them about your quest?	Turn to **101**
Say that you are from another world?	Turn to **73**
Tell them that you are the last survivor of an ambushed caravan?	Turn to **322**
Pretend that you are deaf and dumb?	Turn to **35**
Demand they escort you to Greyguilds-on-the-Moor?	Turn to **95**

66

'Here's your share of the loot, you insolent dog', shouts the biggest thug, attempting to bury his sword in your stomach. You jump aside and meet the attack of the two bruisers. As you do so, the weaselly thief mercilessly kills the jeweller. You must fight both thieves.

	SKILL	STAMINA
First THIEF	6	7
Second THIEF	5	6

If you kill the first thief, turn to **320**.

67

The rolling shield eludes your grasp. The Dragon chuckles and exhales a mighty breath. As the air rushes from its cavernous lungs, it ignites. You are consumed by rolling jets of flame and charred to a cinder. Turn to **43**.

68

You run across the rough ground towards the Orcs, drawing your sword. Unfortunately, as you close with them their Captain, a huge and hulking Orc with yellowed tusks, crashes into you. You grab him but lose your balance and topple over the edge of the chasm. You fall for what seems like an eternity. At least you won't die alone.

69

You climb on, gasping for breath in the thin air. At last you reach the flat summit. The panorama is incredible. The whole plateau lies below you like a table, a collage of tropical forests, mountains and huge lakes, which glisten in the sun. Thirty metres away is a rectangle of shimmering silver, hanging in the air, unsupported. You realize that this is the portal. As you step towards it you hear the rushing of wind. Looking up you see the ancient Red Dragon coming in to land beside the portal. Outside its lair the Dragon is even more impressive and fearsome: warmth and power seem to radiate from its body. 'I am bound by the Gods to guard the portal,' it says in its rich, mellow voice. Will you:

Run to attack the Dragon?	Turn to **382**
Tell him that Death threatens the world?	Turn to **358**
Threaten it?	Turn to **275**

70

Her eyebrows rise in surprise. All four of them look at you doubtfully. The Priest pauses, then says, 'It is the truth and spoken from a true heart.' The Shield-maiden lowers the bow and turns to guard the entrance of the cavern.

'What are we to do? The exits are blocked and I only have enough power to teleport one of us out now,' asks the man in gold.

The man with the glittering sword, a Paladin, says gravely, 'Then we will die together, Wizard, and they will pay dearly.'

'But what of the Talisman?' asks the Priest. 'Perhaps this warrior has been sent by the gods to continue the quest?' Sensing the goodness in these people you wait to hear how you can aid them. Turn to **100**.

71

You walk down the tunnel which soon leads into a circular room of bare stone. In the centre stands a small round pillar. The tunnel continues on the other side of the room. Will you:

Examine the pillar?	Turn to **184**
Go straight through to the tunnel opposite?	Turn to **204**
Return to where the tunnels crossed and choose again?	Turn to **42**

72

A deep dry moat and spiked palisade surround several elegant wattle-and-clay buildings. You are led through the village to what must be the Head-hog's dwelling: a two-storeyed building, part of which is built out of crumbling green stone. A huge mud wallow lies nearby. The Headhog sits on a carved stone throne, his muscles rippling under his blue-black skin. He wears a red robe fastened at his thick neck with a necklace of amber. He introduces himself as the lord of the plateau and you are pleased to discover that you can understand his guttural language quite easily. He seems at ease and, thanking you for the ruby, asks if there is anything you wish to know about the plateau. You ask him about the portals of Mount Star-reach. Turn to **110**.

73

The Captain's brow furrows as you tell your story. There is some muttering from her companions, which she silences with a quick gesture. 'We must take you to Hawkana, in Greyguilds. She will want to speak with you. Climb up behind Elvira here, and give me your sword.' She points to one of the younger women. Will you hand over your sword and get on the horse (turn to **155**), or refuse, saying that you would rather make your own way (turn to **142**)?

74

You stumble off through the darkness, looking for somewhere safer to rest. At last you see an empty stable. You bed down in the straw. Turn to **91**.

75

'We have no time to dally with the likes of you,' says the man in gold. Turning to his companions, he continues. 'What are we to do? The exits are blocked and I have only enough power to teleport one of us out now.'

The man with the glittering sword, a Paladin, says gravely, 'Then we will die together, Wizard, and they will pay dearly.'

'But what of the Talisman?' asks the Priest. 'Perhaps we can use this warrior to continue the quest.' He steps forward and, before you can act, casts a spell. You feel a trance coming over you – the man has hypnotized you – and you tell them everything. Lose 1 LUCK point. Turn to **114**.

76

Hawkana draws her sword and advances on you, snarling with tigerish ferocity. You have just enough time to take out the Vial of Vapours of Speed and inhale. There seems to be no effect – the alchemist has sold you fresh air! With the speed of a cobra Hawkana is upon you and her sword pierces your arm as you drop the empty vial. Lose 2 STAMINA points. If you are still alive you must fight the High Priestess.

HAWKANA   SKILL 12   STAMINA 14

If you win, go to 44.

77

You both walk towards the portal. Suddenly the old man grasps you round the chest. Before you know what is happening he reverts to his normal form, that of a Red Dragon. You are held tightly in his powerful claws. 'You foolish man-thing, never trust a dragon.' So saying, he bites off your head and tosses your corpse down the mountainside. Turn to 43.

78

After a short delay, you are taken into a large office. Inside is a tall, striking, raven-haired woman, dressed in a long black cloak which parts to reveal the polished hilt of a longsword. Her bearing suggests great personal power. She stands and greets you. 'I am Hawkana, High Priestess of the temple of Fell-Kyrinla and Marshal of the Watch. You have been telling some unusual stories.' She nods and the guards begin to search you. You try to resist but are held powerless. The Talisman is ripped from its place of concealment and handed to Hawkana. She recognizes it immediately, and she laughs with rapturous delight. She turns away and says, 'I am going to the temple. Throw this fool out into the street.' You are hustled out and the door of the watch-house slams shut behind you. You have lost the Talisman! What will you do next:

Go back down Guard Street to Store Street?	Turn to 357
Turn down Smith Street?	Turn to 303
Walk down the Street of Seven Sins?	Turn to 264

79

The shield is wrenched from your grasp. Realizing that without it you have no chance, you make a desperate dive for it as it rolls across the rocks. *Test your Luck.* If you are Lucky, turn to 58. If you are Unlucky, turn to 67.

80

You take the right-hand tunnel which soon turns left. You come out into a bare stone room with a small square pillar in the centre. The tunnel continues on the other side of the room. Will you:

Examine the pillar?	Turn to 302
Go straight through to the tunnel opposite?	Turn to 260
Return to where the tunnels crossed and choose again?	Turn to 42

81

'Lies,' it hisses, and strikes you with its claw before you can move. A chill numbness spreads from the wound and you feel as if your life-blood is being drained away. Lose 1 SKILL and 2 STAMINA points. Now you must fight the MINION OF DEATH. Each time it strikes you, you lose 1 SKILL point as well as the normal STAMINA loss.

MINION
OF DEATH   SKILL 7   STAMINA 7

If you win, turn to 175.

82

Drawing back your arm you throw the heavy spear, Dragonsbane, with all your might. Unfortunately, it glances off the heavily armoured scales of the Dragon's back. The Dragon awakes and its yellow slitted eyes hold yours. 'Who are you?' it asks. Fear grips you. You stutter a reply as the Dragon draws a deep breath. Turn to **146**.

83

Have you been told about the storm-drain? If you have, turn to **183**. If not, turn to **149**.

84

You take the smallest feather you can find as a memento of your monumental battle and hurry down the steep mountainside. You reach the bottom of the mountain some hours later and set off across the wilderness once more, towards the plateau which looms ahead. You spend the night in a copse of rowan trees and you wake feeling ready to scale the plateau. Add 2 STAMINA points and turn to **20**.

85

Turning down Silver Street, you are startled by what sounds like men's voices, whispering near by. You soon realize that a trick of the wind is carrying their words to you through a broken piece of pipe, which connects a ramshackle house to an open drain. There are three of them and it seems that they are planning to rob the jeweller's, which you can plainly see on the bend of Silver Street. There is a shabby staircase leading up to the house, and you creep towards it. Will you:

Go up the staircase?	Turn to **245**
Walk quickly to the jeweller's?	Turn to **278**
Ignore this and turn into Store Street?	Turn to **243**

You straddle the Griffin's back. It leaps into the air and takes flight towards the plateau. It flies strongly, higher and higher. The rush of the wind and the sensation of flight is exhilarating. After a few hours the plateau gives way to a thick prehistoric rain forest. Suddenly the Griffin caws a warning. A giant flying reptile is diving to the attack. It crashes into the Griffin, forcing you to lose your grip. You drop some twelve metres but, luckily, a giant fern breaks your fall. You are up to your waist in a pool of water which has collected in the centre of the fern's giant fronds. The flying reptile, a Pteranodon, leaves the Griffin and flies towards you. You must fight it.

PTERANODON   SKILL 7   STAMINA 15

If you win turn to 4.

87

You touch the Amulet as Hawkana draws her sword and advances, snarling with tigerish ferocity. It is an Amulet of Strength against Evil and it increases your SKILL by 2 points, in this battle only. With the speed of a cobra Hawkana is upon you. You must fight the High Priestess.

HAWKANA   SKILL 12   STAMINA 14

If you win, go to 44.

88

The barman says, 'You're not like my usual customers. A rough lot comes in here, most days. These fellows don't rely on charity for a crust, you know.' Will you try to make friends and ask him how he keeps order (turn to 119), or ask him how they get their money (turn to 102)?

89

You walk down the tunnel which turns right again. As you round the corner you hear an ominous sound from the room you have just left. You dart back to see the room filling with sand, and a slab of rock coming down over the entrance. It slams to the floor with a crash and then all is quiet. You can only go on. Turn to **120**.

90

He orders you to leave the village, never to return. He directs you north towards an old temple to Nil, the God who gave rise to the awful progeny known as the Sons of Nil, or Sons of the Void. You thank him and hurriedly leave the village. As soon as you have left it some way behind you, turn back towards Mount Star-reach. Turn to **14**.

You fall into deep slumber and then begin to dream. The Paladin crusader you saw in the Rift appears to you and seems to be giving advice. The shimmering that once limned his sword now surrounds him like a halo. He urges you to enlist the help of the Thieves' Guild, 'though it grieves me to suggest you should have dealings with such people. You may find them in the Red Dragon Inn. They may help you to recover the Talisman from Fell-Kyrinla's temple, where it now lies.' Suddenly the dream seems even more real and the Paladin is shouting, 'Awake, awake! You are in grave danger.' You wake; everything is silent. By the light of the moon you see tendrils of mist curling round the door-jamb. The door crashes open. A pall of mist spills into the stable and a warrior clad in full plate armour, as black as night, and wielding a cruelly spiked mace steps forward. He raises his visor. You can see nothing inside the helmet. Your gaze is held. Now it seems you are looking upon the fires of hell. You are filled with despair as the black mace is raised to crush you. You must fight the DEATH-KNIGHT.

DEATH-KNIGHT   SKILL 10   STAMINA 15

If your STAMINA is reduced to 6 or below, turn to **193**. If you win turn to **62**.

92

'Well if you won't trust me you must go your own way,' he says brusquely. 'If you have lost something and wish to regain it you should contact the Thieves' Guild. That type often frequents the Red Dragon Inn, on the Street of Seven Sins.' You thank him and gather up your belongings. As you leave he calls after you, 'And don't come back, you'll only bring trouble.' You go on your way wondering whether you have made a mistake: could he have helped you? You check your belongings and to your surprise find a pouch you have never seen before, containing five gold pieces. Will you go to the Red Dragon Inn (turn to 57), or head for the temple to Fell-Kyrinla (turn to 221)?

93

The wind whips under your shield and you only just manage to keep your grip on it. You run to attack before the Dragon can cast any more spells. Turn to 382.

94

You have subdued the Griffin, which crouches on the ground before you. You are surprised to hear it speak. 'Spare me, and I will bear you whither you will.' Will you tell it to carry you to the plateau (turn to 86), or leave it and head south-east, away from the hills (turn to 287)?

95

The Captain sneers at you and says sarcastically, 'Why yes, mighty warrior, we shall be glad to do as you ask. You shall dine with our leader, Hawkana, tonight. Mount yourself behind Elvira here,' she says, pointing at one of the younger women. The women begin to chuckle and then the Captain says, 'But first we must take your weapon.' Turn to **142**.

96

You catch it by surprise and strike it a mighty blow. It hisses in rage and pain and comes at you with its claws. You must fight the MINION OF DEATH. Each time it strikes you, it draws your life-force, so you lose 1 SKILL point, as well as the normal STAMINA loss.

MINION
OF DEATH   SKILL 7   STAMINA 5

If you win, turn to **175**.

You have run into the gothic building you saw from the road. It is the temple of Death and a huge congregation is taking part in a religious ceremony. Hundreds of black-cowled figures kneel at prayer in the dark, vaulted church. The black candles shed enough light for you to see that many of them have embraced Death already. Quickly, you swathe yourself in one of the black robes of worship hanging by the arch. The organ sounds a loud and doleful chord and the high priest, Somnus, is invited to begin. He raises his arms and his voice echoes round the vaults as he chants an invocation in the same doleful tones. The altar is suffused with red light and a phantom lake of boiling blood appears. Emerging from the lake are six mounted wraiths, hunched figures cloaked in a pall of evil. The blood pours from them as they spur their black hell-steeds into the aisle. Somnus cries, 'I charge you, Instruments of Death, to recover the Talisman!' In unison the long-dead lords reply, their voices harsh with the hatred of ages, 'It shall be done.' The congregation sighs with a mixture of fear and awe. You notice one of them walking to the back of the church where he places a helmet on his head and disappears completely. Will you:

Melt into the congregation and kneel down?	Turn to **157**
Make a run for the door?	Turn to **188**
Put on one of the helmets?	Turn to **165**

You tell him everything and he listens with growing amazement. He introduces himself as Apothecus, a sage of history. 'I have heard of the Talisman of Death. You must recover it at all costs.' He suggests that you enlist the help of the Thieves' Guild, as he doesn't think you can recapture it alone. 'It will be in the temple to Fell-Kyrinla by now, I'll warrant. Hawkana, the High Priestess, will be holding it there. Go to the Red Dragon Inn on the Street of Seven Sins. It is dangerous, but you may make contact with the thieves there.' He gives you a breakfast of savoury pancakes and invites you to dinner that evening, saying that he will try to discover more to aid you. 'In the meantime,' he says, 'take these.' He hands you five pieces of gold and a ring. 'It is a ring which increases your skill at arms.' Add 1 to your SKILL score while wearing this ring. As you leave he gives you a jade rose. 'When you return this evening show this and I will know that you are not a shape-changer.' You thank him for his help and leave the bungalow. Will you go to the Red Dragon Inn (turn to **57**), or head for the temple (turn to **221**)?

99

You continue along the wall and, to your relief, find the postern gate. You duck through and out into the night beyond. Gain 1 LUCK point for escaping the city. Turn to **8**.

100

The Priest steps towards you and tells you this story. 'Long ago the minions of the God Death, in the City of the Runes of Doom, fashioned a Talisman that would allow them, if the time was right, to summon their God to the surface of this world. That time has now come. If Death is summoned all life will cease. Only Death's minions will continue to exist in an awful half-life. His presence will spread like a grey shadow across the world of Orb. Everything will turn to dust and the balance of nature will be disrupted for ever. The Loremasters of Serakub, a group of holy people, have striven to prevent this. They sent a group of Crusaders, of which we four alone survive, on a quest to steal the Talisman. The Fleshless King of the minions of Death had sent the Talisman to the depths of the Rift for safe-keeping.

We have entered this pit of evil and seized it.' He pulls a necklace out from under his surcoat. On it hangs a disc of obsidian, in the middle of which is a skull carved in ruby – the Talisman of Death! He hands it to you. 'Here. For the sake of all Orb you must take this Talisman and continue the quest. It cannot be destroyed, but if you can take it to your world, it will be beyond the reach of the claw of the Fleshless King.'

You are impressed by the courage and unselfish fortitude of these people and resolve to continue the quest. You take the Talisman. It feels cold and heavy around your neck. The Wizard turns to you and says, 'I am going to use the powers of magic to transport you to the surface. Head west until you come to the city of learning, Greyguilds-on-the-Moor, where you may discover a way to return to your own world. Do not fail us! Here, take this gold, it may be of use.' He gives you a purse with 10 gold pieces in it. As the Wizard prepares his spell, a horde of creatures boils into the cavern. Turn to **125**.

101

The Captain and other members of the patrol start to laugh at you. She throws her head back with her hands on her hips and stares at you. 'Give me your sword and climb up behind Elvira here.' She points to one of the younger women. 'We must take you back to Greyguilds.' Will you hand your sword to her (turn to 155), or refuse to give it up (turn to 142)?

102

The surly men around the ale cellar scowl at you. The barman says, 'Don't know I'm sure. Why don't you ask them?' and then shuts up. One of the men at the table of six says menacingly, 'Yes, come on and ask us.' Turn to 280.

103

You roll through just as the rock slams down with a reverberating crash, inches from your face. You walk down the tunnel until you come to a dark iron door. A message has been painted in shimmering letters upon it – 'One only can be read.' You swing the door open and enter a rectangular room with an iron door in each wall. In the centre of the room stand three pillars, one rectangular, one circular and one square. Will you:

Leave the room through one of the other doors?	Turn to **339**
Examine the rectangular pillar?	Turn to **290**
Examine the circular pillar?	Turn to **321**
Examine the square pillar?	Turn to **345**

104

You continue on down Smith Street. There are no shops here and the street is deserted except for a stooping, cowled figure, who looks like a beggar. He comes up to you and suddenly draws himself up to his full height. Inside the cowl there is nothing – no face, just two glowing coals suspended in blackness. Your horror at this apparition turns to dread as it hisses in a sibilant whisper, 'Did you think you could run from Death? Give me the Talisman.' A black-gloved claw reaches out towards you. Do you say that you no longer have the Talisman (turn to **81**), or attack this thing immediately (turn to **96**)?

105

You jump aside at the last moment but are still caught by the heat of the blast. Lose 3 STAMINA points. If you are still alive you may wish to use one of the following, if you have any of them:

A Vial of Vapours of Speed	Turn to **76**
An Amulet made from the Horn of a Unicorn	Turn to **87**
A Scroll of Agonizing Doom	Turn to **59**
None of these things	Turn to **50**

The magician conjures up a cloud of blue, green and pink smoke, which engulfs the spectators. While you watch, Tyutchev, the man from the Red Dragon Inn, appears from the shadows and enters the smoke. By the time it clears neither he nor the magician in the grey robes are anywhere to be seen, but the members of the crowd are accusing one another, between coughing fits, of being cutpurses. You realize that Tyutchev and the magician are in cahoots. As you turn to leave, a servant places a silver salver under your nose. It bears a gold-embossed card inviting you to take sherry with one Mortphilio. 'This way if you please,' says the man. You ask who Mortphilio is and he replies, 'One of the elders of the city,' but says no more. Will you go with him (turn to **144**), or decline the invitation (turn to **83**)?

107

You walk off in the opposite direction. Your leg aches where the man-trap wounded you and you cannot find an inn. Unable to go any further, you curl up in an alley and sleep, despite the cold. Your awakening is rude indeed, for you are being dangled in front of the face of a huge OGRE! He grins evilly as he swings your head against the wall and drops you. Lose 2 STAMINA points. If you are still alive you must fight the Ogre.

OGRE   SKILL 8   STAMINA 10

If you win, turn to 74.

108

You wake up with a start. It is dawn. You regain any STAMINA points you lost fighting Hawkana in the spirit world. However, you feel as if you had actually fought her and your sleep has had no restorative powers. You gather up your belongings and trudge onward. Turn to 326.

109

Your spirit floats gently towards the Valley of Death. The featureless, wind-blasted plain stretches away endlessly, beyond the horizon. The souls of the dead wander there aimlessly, in solitude. Just as you approach the edge of the valley, an ethereal wind gets up and your soul is wafted away. Soon you feel yourself in the presence of the two who summoned you to this fantastic world of magic. The eyeless being in robes of shifting hues says, 'All is not yet lost.' You understand the words without hearing them. 'If your spirit is willing we will reunite it with your body and turn back the wheels of time.' The other being offers you a choice: 'If you wish it, I will send you back in time. You will be at the lip of the Rift again.' Do you wish to go back in time to attempt the quest again? If you do, he lays a hand on your shoulder. They disappear. You are alive again. Your wounds are healed and you have 10 Provisions. You have only the equipment with which you began the adventure, including the Talisman of Death, if you had lost it. Anything else you picked up on the way has disappeared and will have to be crossed off your Adventure Sheet. Your SKILL, STAMINA and LUCK are at their *Initial* levels. Suddenly you are on the surface of Orb once again. Turn to **125**.

110

The Hoglord says, 'I will help you, man-thing, for you may help me. An ancient Red Dragon has its lair within Mount Star-reach. It is the guardian of the portals. The last time it awoke, which was before my children were born, it despoiled our villages. You must slay it before you can go through the portals. It breathes fire which one cannot withstand, save when one is sheltered by scales from the Dragon itself. You must steal three of the scales from its lair and fashion a shield out of them.' He gives you a parting gift, a stoppered gourd containing the Gum of an Amber Pine, with which to make the shield. You dine with them on mangoes, nuts and guavas (gain 2 STAMINA points). You thank them and leave. After a long climb you come to a wide cave mouth reeking of sulphur – the Dragon's lair. You decide to enter. Turn to **7**.

111

When they see that you have overcome their leader single-handed, the rest of the Orcs turn tail and run. You hurry on down the far side of the hill. Before you lies a steep-sided valley deep in ferns. You decide to head down into it, hoping to elude the Elves. Turn to **203**.

112

The wind whirls under your shield, whips it out of your grasp and, to your dismay, hurls it over the summit. The Dragon chuckles and exhales a mighty breath. As the air rushes from its cavernous lungs it ignites. You are consumed by rolling jets of flame and charred to a cinder. Turn to **43**.

113

You step over the fallen guard and, pushing open the double doors, enter the Inner Sanctum of the temple. A tall raven-haired woman, Hawkana, the High Priestess, is praying at the altar, upon which lies the Talisman of Death. Beyond the altar is a large marble statue of the Goddess wearing chain-mail, her expression arrogant and cruelly beautiful. Hawkana rises and turns. She resembles the statue and is wearing a long dress of black chainmail. Turn to **222**.

114

The Priest steps towards you and tells you this story. 'Long ago the minions of the God Death, in the City of the Runes of Doom, fashioned a Talisman that would allow them, when the time suited their evil designs, to summon their God to the surface of this world. That time has now come. If Death is summoned, all life will cease. Only Death's minions will continue to exist in an awful half-life. His presence will spread like a grey shadow across the world of Orb, which is where you are now. Everything will turn to dust and the balance of nature will be disrupted for ever. The Loremasters of Serakub, a group of holy people, have striven to prevent this. They sent a group of Crusaders, of which we four alone survive, on a quest to steal the Talisman. The Fleshless King of the minions of Death had sent the Talisman to the depths of the Rift for safe-keeping. We have entered this pit of evil

and seized it.' He pulls out a necklace from under his surcoat. On it hangs a disc of obsidian, with a ruby skull carved at its centre – the Talisman of Death! He hands it to you. 'Here. For the sake of all Orb you must take this Talisman and continue the quest. It cannot be destroyed but, if you can return to your own world with it, it will be beyond the reach of the claw of the Fleshless King.'

The hypnotic spell binds you – your whole being is given over to the completing of the quest. The Talisman feels cold and heavy around your neck. The Wizard turns to you and says, 'I am going to use the powers of magic to transport you to the surface. Head west until you come to the city of learning, Greyguilds-on-the-Moor, where you may discover a way to return to your own world. Do not fail us! Here, take this gold, it may be of use.' He gives you a purse with 10 gold pieces in it. As the Wizard prepares his spell, a horde of creatures boils into the cavern. Turn to **125**.

115

You tiptoe stealthily towards the Dragon. Its nostrils twitch and a great yellow slitted eye flutters open and fixes you with its gaze. Will you:

Run out of the cavern and up the mountain as fast as you can?	Turn to 335
Stand your ground?	Turn to 170
Run back, hoping to explore the narrow side-tunnel?	Turn to 22

116

You trudge on beneath oppressive grey skies. The Talisman seems to weigh you down, like a millstone round your neck. At last you can see the plateau looming ahead of you, but this does nothing to dispel the nervousness you feel. At dusk you make camp and the dark pall of night engulfs you. Exhausted, you fall asleep. A more vivid dream disturbs your rest. Hawkana appears again, but her outline is hazy and insubstantial. She beckons once more – the void that separates you is neither time nor space. You feel yourself moving towards her and everything around you becomes misty and ethereal. You have been drawn to the edge of the Valley of Death. You must fight her.

HAWKANA'S SPIRIT	SKILL 10	STAMINA 12

If you win, turn to 108. If you lose this combat in the spirit world, turn to 23.

117

You walk with the Priestess into a small grassy square. On the far side of the square stands a magnificent tiered temple, covered by a wonderful hanging garden. A flock of many types of small coloured birds takes flight as you pass two guards and enter through the wide green doors. Inside is a long hall, decorated with flowers. You both kneel in prayer before the altar, which is loaded with grain and fruit. She prays for the protection of all living things. After a few moments of reflection, she takes your hand in hers and leads you into a small room at the side of the hall. On a stand is a suit of silvery chainmail. Lillantha says, 'The All-Mother has spoken to me of your quest. She wishes you to take this – it may be of help.' Thanking her, you put on the chainmail which is miraculously light. It is obviously magical – gain 1 SKILL point. 'One final thing: the gates are guarded by followers of the All-Mother on the evenings of market-days and for the three days following. If you wish to leave the city without others knowing, leave then.' You thank her and, leaving the peace of the temple, return to the hubbub of Store Street. Turn to **130**.

118

You have come under the Dragon's spell. He urges you to approach the portal. When you get closer he says, 'You man-things are so easily tricked.' He jumps upon you and rends you limb from limb. Turn to **43**.

'I manage, mostly,' he says; 'but it puts me in mind of one time not so long ago when things really got out of hand.' He goes on to tell you a story about Heimdol the Mighty. It seems that Heimdol was one of the strongest and most unpleasant men ever to have swilled beer in the Red Dragon. One day a stranger, Tyutchev, accepted his invitation to a bout of arm-wrestling. Heimdol lost for the first time in his life. He was furious and threatened awful reprisals if Tyutchev ever returned. A few nights later Tyutchev did return and began methodically to insult Heimdol and two of his friends. In the inevitable fight which followed Tyutchev killed them all and carved his initials on Heimdol's forehead. 'He worships the God of insane chaos, Anarchil, and since then none has dared gainsay him here, even though they are all thieves and murderers.' You decide the time has come to introduce yourself to the thieves, and you walk over to their table. Turn to **280**.

120

You walk down the tunnel until you come to a dark iron door. A message has been painted in shimmering letters upon it – 'One only may be read.' You swing the door open and enter a rectangular room with iron doors in each wall. In the centre of the room stand three small pillars, one rectangular, one circular and one square. Will you:

Leave the room through one of the other doors?	Turn to **339**
Examine the rectangular pillar?	Turn to **290**
Examine the circular pillar?	Turn to **321**
Examine the square pillar?	Turn to **345**

121

You sleep again, until the late morning sun, shining into the stable, wakes you. You stretch and your hand touches something cold lying in the straw. It is a gold piece, which you decide to pocket before leaving the stable. If you want to go down one of the side-streets that leads to the Street of Seven Sins and the Red Dragon Inn, turn to **57**. If you decide against mixing with thieves and try to take the Talisman from the temple on your own, turn to **221**.

122

They accept the ruby, showing their appreciation with bows and snorts. In a friendly manner they motion you to go with them to their village. Will you thank them, but decline and go on your way (turn to 14), or accompany them to their village (turn to 72)?

123

The arrogance of the warrior-women is ruffled at your mention of the City of the Runes of Doom. The Captain hesitates, narrowing her eyes. There is a flicker of fear in the eyes of some of the younger women. The Captain clears her throat and says, 'We must take you to Hawkana, Marshal of the Watch at Greyguilds.' Turn to 152.

124

The guards come back down the stairs and you are attacked from all sides. You fight valiantly but there are too many of them. You are overwhelmed and slain. Turn to 109.

125

Dark Elves and Cave Trolls are pouring into the cavern, attacking the Shieldmaiden. As the Paladin and Priest rush to her aid, you see a huge shadowy form looming behind the sea of Elves and Trolls. The Paladin's glittering sword cuts through the horde but the Dark Elves are using magic and the Shieldmaiden is unable to turn back their attack. She falls beneath their onslaught. The huge fiend howls triumphantly, just as the wizard completes his spell. Turn to **185**.

126

At nightfall you set off for the Moorgate hoping that the followers of the All-Mother will now be on guard. As you leave Store Street, a figure steps from the shadows. He wears a hood which conceals his features but you recognize the ornately spiked armour and black-steel sword of a Dark Elf. One of those who attacked the Crusaders in the Rift must have infiltrated the city! He doesn't waste words but swings his sword. You must fight the Dark Elf.

DARK ELF   skill 8   stamina 8

If you win, turn to **249**.

You force yourself on through the wilds of nature's creation. But the singing of the birds sounds hollow to you and premonitions of death haunt you as you stumble on in a waking dream. At nightfall you build a large fire and set torches around it. Unable to sleep, you wait and listen. The Talisman grows heavy. Soon the wild neighing which disturbed your sleep yesterday peals again, rending the peace of the night. The chilling challenge is answered, again and again. Soon, to your horror, six of the nightmarish horses, eyes and nostrils aflame, appear, each bearing the crooked, life-hating spirit of a Wraith. They form an arc, all staring at you intently. In unison their cracked voices cry, 'We are the instruments of Death. We have come to claim you for our master and to take back his Talisman.' You stand with the fire between yourself and them, but they urge their horses through the flames. Under their attack you feel your life-force ebbing away. You become like them, a travesty of life, for ever doomed to an existence filled with hatred and jealousy of all living things.

128

You are left alone to wonder how the law-keepers of this city could be so cruel as to leave an innocent person in such dire straits. You tear feverishly at the trap, terrified of some footpad slitting your throat for his own vile amusement. Soft footsteps approach. You look over your shoulder and see a man approaching. 'Here,' he says, 'let me rescue you from this trap.' He steps on the release catch, which had been out of your reach and the trap springs open. You step free and he walks along by your side. 'Have you a place to stay tonight? Perhaps you would like to sleep in my humble abode?' he asks, looking sideways at you. You are curious that he should be walking the streets alone at night, but you are also exhausted. Will you accept his offer and go home with him (turn to **143**), or decline his offer (turn to **107**)?

129

You realize that the Dragon is beguiling you and that you should never allow a Dragon to engage you in conversation. You run forward to attack him. Turn to **382**.

As you walk along Store Street once more, you
notice that the stores are closing. The throng of
people hurrying home parts, to make way for a large
black carriage drawn by two black mares. They carry
plumed headdresses made of long black feathers.
The cloaked coachman stares grimly ahead. You
step into the gutter to let the coach pass and, as you
do so, the coachman reins in. Inside you see an
empty black coffin, but the name inscribed in silver
letters on the lid is your own. The door of the funeral
carriage opens and a handsome man with a silver
cane steps down. He is dressed in the finest silver
satin and sable furs. A storekeeper greets him. He
smiles and nods, then turns to you. 'I am the envoy
of Death; I have come for the Talisman,' he says in a
voice of doom. As you prepare to resist, a startling
transformation takes place, which seems to be
ignored by all around. His magnificent furs turn to
rags. Where once blue eyes looked out from a finely
featured face, now hollow sockets gaze at you from
a blackened and cracked skull. His skeletal hand
now grips a tarnished rapier. You realize that no-
body else can see this transformation. 'Give it to
me,' he says. Will you:

Give him the Talisman (if you have it)?	Turn to **179**
Attack him immediately?	Turn to **271**
Deny that you have it?	Turn to **220**

131

Realizing that you cannot stay with the Sage, you set out to find a bed for the night. Turn to **28**.

132

You are engulfed in flame. The pain is terrible and you can hardly see. Lose 6 STAMINA points. If you are still alive you may wish to use one of the following, if you have any of them:

Vapours of Speed	Turn to **76**
Unicorn Amulet	Turn to **87**
Scroll of Agonizing Doom	Turn to **59**
None of these things	Turn to **50**

133

Deduct one unit of Provisions from your Adventure Sheet. Too late, you realize you are handing them salted pork. The Hogmen are offended. They demand in grunts that you go with them to their village. Will you go with them (turn to **365**), or refuse (turn to **172**)?

134

You set off across the rocky broken ground towards the hills. After a short while you notice two armed bands running towards you. The group to the south consists of twenty or more Orcs, snarling as they lope purposefully towards you. They are hunched and misshapen, dressed in greasy, blackened leather and carrying saw-toothed scimitars. Their shields are emblazoned with a purple claw. To the north, you can make out a small group of Dark Elves, similar to those which killed the Shieldmaiden. They are tall and lithe, wearing ornately spiked armour and carrying longswords of a dull black metal. They are some way off but are closing fast. Will you:

Head for the Orcs?	Turn to **68**
Head for the Elves?	Turn to **214**
Run for the hills?	Turn to **63**
Hide?	Turn to **148**

135

Treading on some dry leaves, you are unlucky to snap a hidden twig. As the BASILISK turns its gaze upon you, your body grows heavy. You fling yourself into the undergrowth as your skin begins to turn a stony grey colour. You have just avoided being turned to stone by the reptile's gaze, but the effects of partial petrification have damaged your muscle fibres. Lose 1 SKILL point. Hastily, you cut a path through the undergrowth and leave the sluggish but deadly monster behind, rejoining the path further on. Turn to **270**.

136

An inscription on the rectangular pillar reads:

Put yourself in the place of the monkey.
To the left is danger; the idle shall act.

As you ponder the meaning of the strange message, a trickle of sand falls on your head. You look up to see the roof cracking and an avalanche of sand starts pouring down. With a grating rumble, a slab of rock starts to fall across the exit ahead. Your only hope is to hurl yourself through the narrowing gap. Roll two dice. If the total is equal to or less than your SKILL score turn to **103**. If the total is greater than your SKILL score turn to **215**.

137

You begin rummaging through the trappings of the temple. You feel a tingling sensation in your finger, followed by a sharp pain. Looking at your hand you see that Hawkana's ring is shrinking. You try to pull it off but it is too late. You can only watch as the ring constricts to a solid ball and severs your finger. Lose 1 SKILL and 2 STAMINA points. You can feel the dreadful malice of the Goddess directed against you and you decide to try the doors. Turn to **16**.

138

You take out the Talisman and examine it carefully. For the first time you notice a glowing inscription, as if the nearness of the minions of Death was lending it power. *I am Death's Talisman. I am protected by the Faceless Ones who serve my wielder.* At nightfall, you build a large fire and set torches around it. Unable to sleep, you wait and listen. The Talisman grows heavy. Soon the wild neighing which disturbed your sleep yesterday peals again, rending the peace of the night. The chilling challenge is answered, again and again. Soon, to your horror, six of the nightmarish horses, eyes and nostrils aflame, appear, each bearing the crooked life-hating spirit of a Wraith. They form an arc, all staring at you intently. In unison, their cracked voices cry, 'We are the instruments of Death. We have come to claim you for our master and to take back his Talisman.' Will you:

Threaten to cast the Talisman into
the fire? **Turn to 388**
Try to break through the circle? **Turn to 164**
Try to use the power of the
Talisman? **Turn to 46**

139

Inside, working at an anvil, is a brawny man, glistening with sweat. He is fashioning the hilt of a sword. Other finished swords stand in a rack along one side of the shop. 'Take your pick. Seven gold pieces,' he says, without looking up. You may buy one if you wish (turn to **160**), or thank him and leave (turn to **104**).

140

You can hear the clank of armour as a group of guards rushes past the arras, heading up the stairs. You continue down until you reach the double doors at the bottom. A guard remains on duty before them. She shouts a warning and runs forward to attack you. You must fight her.

TEMPLE GUARD   SKILL 7   STAMINA 8

If she is still alive after five combat rounds, turn to **124**. If you win within five combat rounds, turn to **113**.

141

Harg disappears before the hammer lands. 'Very good,' says Thaum. 'Now, what about this?' Turn to **171**.

142

At a command from the Captain, the circle of horses closes in on you. You draw your sword and manage to wound one of the women before you are attacked from all sides. They are strong fighters and use the flat blades of their swords to stun you. You drop your sword and fall to the ground. Lose 2 SKILL points. When you acquire another sword, you may restore them. There are too many warriors to resist, so you decide to do as you are told for a while and accept a helping hand on to Elvira's horse. She does not look too pleased that you are going to sit behind her all the way to Greyguilds. You console yourself with the thought that at least you are going in the right direction. Turn to **257**.

143

The man's house is a small stone bungalow. He leads you into his bedroom and offers you a straw-filled mattress behind a curtain. Thankful for the chance to rest, you go to sleep without asking any questions. You sleep deeply and regain 4 STAMINA points. You wake to find that your host is sitting watching you. 'I hope you are well rested. You talked in your sleep.' He smiles at you and says, 'Do you need help? Has someone stolen something from you? How did you come to be trapped, alone on the street late at night?' If you want to tell him the whole story and ask him for advice, turn to **98**. If you would prefer to say that you cannot answer, turn to **92**.

144

You are led along tree-lined avenues, through a quarter of the city you have not yet visited. Ahead of you is a large gothic building with pinnacles surmounted by bat-like gargoyles. Before you reach it, the servant leads you into a nearby house. You follow him through to a dark parlour at the back.

The walls are made of pale bamboo and in a gloomy corner a decrepit-looking invalid is sitting in a bath-chair, most of his form hidden under blankets. The servant lights four large black candles before leaving you alone with Mortphilio. 'Thank you for coming. It is seldom that I entertain anyone who looks so vital and full of life.' His voice is hoarse and he finds it an effort to speak. The smoke from the candles makes you feel sleepy, but you are startled back to full awareness when a human skull on the mantelpiece starts to talk. 'This is the one, master.' At a command from Mortphilio, the skull lifts off the mantelpiece and hovers, shadowy wings holding it aloft. 'Kill,' says the necromancer and the skull hurtles towards you, jaws snapping. You must fight the WINGED SKULL

WINGED SKULL   SKILL 7   STAMINA 6

If you win turn, to 396.

145

Scarface says, 'What do you mean? Are you suggesting we are thieves?' There is an edge in his voice and a tension among his comrades, two of whom have their hands upon their daggers. Will you:

Hotly deny it?	Turn to 272
Say that you are?	Turn to 281
Ignore this, and say you have valuable information for them?	Turn to 246

146

The Dragon exhales a mighty breath. As the air rushes from its lungs it ignites and rolling jets of flame fill the cavern. You are charred to a cinder. Turn to **43**.

147

You hide in the middle of a clump of bushes and peer out into the clearing. After a while, the Druid reappears in front of you. 'Since you have chosen to further defile the Sacred Grove by remaining here, I shall assume you have no wish to leave.' Before you can move, he utters some strange words and the bushes begin to grow around you. The leafy tendrils which wrap themselves around your limbs are surprisingly tough. You are held fast. You plead with him to free you but to no avail. After three days without water you slip from delirium into a coma, from which you never recover.

148
You dart down a gully and conceal yourself as best you can in a crack in the rock that reeks of sulphur, hoping that the stream of pebbles you dislodged will not give you away. Soon you can hear the ominous sounds of snuffling as the Orcs try to sniff you out. Suddenly one of them cries out – you have been discovered! You struggle out of your hiding-place and draw your sword but you are bowled over in the rush. One of them grabs your pouch of gold. The coins fly out into the air. Immediately they begin to squabble over the spoils. They do not notice that the group of Elves have appeared at the top of the gully and are looking down. Without a word, the five Elves descend upon the Orcs and, thanks to their magic, soon prevail. Seizing your opportunity, you grab your empty pouch and flee over the hill into the valley beyond. Turn to **203**.

149

You turn left down Hornbeam Road, looking for the coal-hole. You see what looks like a coal-cellar at the back of a dilapidated warehouse. You duck into it and find a small crawl-way hidden on the other side of the pile of coal. You crawl down a chute and out into a small passageway that winds for some distance beneath the city. You come to a door and push it open. You step into a magnificently furnished room; evidently the Thieves' Guild lacks nothing. A group of men is waiting for you, lounging on sofas. Some of them you recognize from the Red Dragon Inn, in particular the one with a scar running from ear to chin. Turn to **209**.

150

'We are the priesthood of Death,' says one of the figures. 'We have come for what is ours.' Your arms are held and you are searched. Realizing that you are not carrying the Talisman, they step back. One of them strikes you across the face. 'Where is it hidden – worm?' Suddenly, the clatter of hooves disturbs the menacing priests. A large group of riders carrying torches comes into sight and the priests melt back into the shadows as silently as they came. The riders of the Watch halt before you. 'You're in a pretty pickle. That's one less problem for us tonight, eh, girls?' This provokes a gale of laughter but you fail to see the funny side as they ride off, leaving you held fast in the jaws of the trap. Turn to **128**.

151

They stare and you cannot be sure what effect your gestures are having, or even if they can understand you at all. Will you:

Offer them some dried meat, if you have any left?	Turn to **133**
Offer them a ruby, if you have one?	Turn to **122**
Attack them?	Turn to **172**

152

The Captain of the patrol demands that you surrender your sword, and says, 'Climb up behind Elvira there.' She points to one of the younger women. Will you obey (turn to **155**), or refuse (turn to **142**)?

153

With a shock, you realize that your foot is poking out under the arras. You pull it back as fast as you can, but you hear footsteps stopping on the other side. A woman's voice rings out, 'Ha! A rat, dead for a silver.' She plunges her sword through the arras and into your stomach. Within moments you are dead. Turn to **109**.

154

As the sun rises, you set off once more across the wild plains. With every hour that passes, the Talisman seems to grow heavier. You realize that it is registering the presence of the minions of Death. Do you wish to examine it again (turn to **138**), or keep it hidden in case it may draw them to you (turn to **127**)?

155

Elvira helps you up behind her. She appears none too pleased at the prospect of sharing her horse with you and you ride in silence across the wilderness. Lose 2 SKILL points until you acquire another sword. Turn to **257**.

156

You come out into the Street of Seven Sins and soon find the Red Dragon Inn. Steps lead downwards and the sound of raucous laughter floats up from the smoke-filled gloom below. You enter and walk over to the only part of the dive where it is light enough to make anything out. Passing tables and stools, you come to the bar, behind which stands the bulky proprietor of the inn. Do you have the brass tiger charm? If you do, turn to **11**. If you do not, turn to **3**.

157

You kneel at the end of a row of worshippers. A golden chalice is being passed along and each member of the congregation drinks from it. Your neighbour drinks with relish and then turns to you; his face is waxen and white, but his eyes are crimson and bloodshot. Blood drips from his vampire fangs. He hands you the chalice and you have to drink. It is human blood, cursed in Death's name. It curdles in your stomach, and you are seized by a palsy and lose 4 STAMINA points. If you are still alive, you see the wraiths ride into the inner chapel, accompanied by Somnus, and the congregation begins to file out. You manage to gain the street without being noticed and, flinging the black robe away, you set out in search of the Thieves' Guild. Turn to **83**.

158

You ask the scholars to use their spell. 'Something appears to be wrong,' mumbles Moreau guiltily. The spell is not working. Out of the corner of your eye you can see him gesticulating as if casting a spell, but the beast is unaffected. You must fight it to the death. Return to the paragraph you came from. You may not appeal for help again.

159

You force through heavy undergrowth for some time, making your way over the hill and into the thick, wooded valley on the other side. You then take a trail heading west and are making good speed until, rounding a corner, you see a huge brown-scaled lizard with eight legs, basking in the sun. Its heavy horned jaw is filled with long pointed teeth. You may *Test your Luck* to see if you can slip past without waking it. If you are Lucky, turn to **267**. If you are Unlucky, turn to **135**. If you prefer not to take this risk and leave the path to cut a way through the undergrowth, turn to **384**.

160

You choose a sword which feels well balanced. It is a well-crafted longsword, similar to those used by the warrior-women. You may restore the 2 SKILL points you lost if you had your sword taken. You pay the man and leave. Turn to 104.

161

Before you plunge your arm into the water, you notice that the sap from the tree is healing a small graze on your wrist. You realize it has healing powers and decide to collect some more sap from the branch you cut from the tree. You may use the Sap of the Willow to restore 4 STAMINA points once, when you think it will help you most. Moving quickly away from the spring you decide to follow the small river that runs through the valley, heading west. Turn to 39.

162

'We are the priesthood of Death,' says one of the figures. 'We have come for what is ours.' Your arms are held and you are searched. The Talisman is torn from you by their leader. 'I have it, brothers, I have it,' he exclaims in triumph. 'Now may our Lord enter his kingdom.' They cheer loudly, oblivious to the approach of a large group of riders. 'Stand, make no move,' a woman's voice rings out. It is the Watch. One of the priests mumbles an unholy incantation. You see a wave of fear break over the women and their steeds. Some cannot control their horses, others flee, but the bravest charge the priests with loud cries of battle. The priests are unprepared: some are knocked to the ground, others make good their escape, as silently as they came. The Talisman falls to the ground, its bearer decapitated as he turns to flee. It is caught up by one of the Watch, who announces her intention of taking it to the temple of Fell-Kyrinla. They wheel their horses and ride away, leaving you to rot. You have lost the Talisman. Cursing bitterly, you resolve that if you escape you will not rest until you have regained it. Turn to **128**.

163

You land safely next to the thieves. Scarface looks surprised to see you. 'Bloodheart?' he inquires. 'Failed, you treacherous dogs,' you reply, brandishing your sword. Jemmy the Rat turns tail and flees across the roof-tops. Lord Min looks at Scarface and shrugs. 'I'm not fighting the killer of Hawkana,' he says. They swing under the eaves and climb like spiders to an open window. Not wishing to attempt this climb, you make your way back to the safe house across the roof-tops, and climb down to the street, where you stop to regain your breath before leaving the city. Turn to **235**.

164

You thrust the torch at the head of one of the nightmarish steeds; the flames flicker, but earthly fire cannot harm them and their riders urge them at you. Under their attack you feel your life-force ebbing away. You become like them, a travesty of life, for ever doomed.

165

Worshippers make way for you as you walk towards the helmet, your face shrouded in the cowl of the black robe. It is standing on a table and is made of interwoven silver bands. You place it in your head and find yourself outside in the street. The helmet bestows quickness of thought and reaction to its wearer. Add 1 to your SKILL score. You guess that powerful Priests of Death use the helmets to come and go from the temple without being seen. Feeling lucky to be alive you set out to find the Thieves' Guild. Turn to **83**.

166

Smiling delightedly, she asks about Wodeman. You tell her what happened in the Sacred Grove. 'Then you are welcome at the temple. I am Lillantha, a Priestess of the All-Mother, Fountain of Life. I am on my way to prayer. Perhaps you would like to join me?' Will you accompany her (turn to **117**), or decline and say you must be on your way (turn to **130**)?

167

Their eyes narrow and suddenly a terrible pain shoots into your kidneys. A thief has crept up silently behind you and knifed you in the back (lose 6 STAMINA points). If you are still alive, you whirl round and back to the bar. You see a wiry young man holding a dagger dripping with your blood. The thieves close in but with your back to the bar only three can attack you. You must fight all three at once.

	SKILL	STAMINA
BACK-STABBER	6	6
SCARFACE	7	9
Second CUT-THROAT	7	8

If you kill Back-stabber and reduce Scarface's STAMINA to 5 or less, turn to **259**.

168

As you touch the door, the SERPENT comes to life. It strikes like lightning, sinking its venomous fangs into your neck. The poison is deadly. You stagger, your blood boiling, but you are paralysed and cannot even inhale. You die of suffocation. Turn to **43**.

169

Two newcomers enter the Red Dragon ale cellar. The first is a very tall, wiry, man whose frame is draped in a black cloak. The only hint of colour is his hair, very curly and dyed bright corn-yellow. The second is a handsome young woman dressed in a bizarre patchwork of armour. The barman mutters under his breath, then forces his face into a smile. 'Tyutchev, Cassandra, welcome!' he shouts obsequiously. The thieves move away from you to sit at another table. Tyutchev strolls to the bar and orders a drink. Cassandra sits opposite you, at your table. She ignores you and Tyutchev joins her. Will you:

Say nothing?	Turn to 2
Get up and leave the ale cellar?	Turn to 363
Introduce yourself?	Turn to 374

170

The Dragon raises its head, 'Good-day to you, manling.' It speaks! Its voice is as soft as honey. It appears to smile and you feel it may be friendly to you. 'Welcome to my lair. Are you looking for something? Can I help?' Will you try to make friends with the Dragon (turn to 317), or tell it of the Talisman and your need to pass through the portal (turn to 356)?

171

While Tyutchev draws his sword, Thaum points at you. From his finger a ball of multi-coloured fire flies towards you. Will you try to avoid the fireball by running at Tyutchev (turn to **244**), or hold your ground (turn to **225**)?

172

They lower their heads and charge at you. You wound two of them before another catches you with his tusks. The tremendous momentum of his charge pitches you on to your back. Lose 2 STAMINA points. If you are still alive, they pin you down and drag you off to their village. Turn to **365**.

173

'Impossible,' snaps the Captain, 'The Spires lie to the west of Greyguilds and you are going towards it not coming away from it. You are under arrest.' Turn to **152**.

174

The Wraith and its hell-steed seem to disappear in the wind. It may be a trick of the wind, but you seem to hear a ghostly voice whispering, 'We shall return.' The Talisman feels lighter again. With a sigh of relief, you lie down to sleep. You awake, feeling better. Gain 2 STAMINA points and restore all but 1 of the SKILL points you have lost fighting the Wraith. Turn to **154**.

175

Your last blow meets no resistance. The grey cloak billows to the ground in a heap. All is silent except for a sudden keening of the wind. You rest and begin to overcome the shock to your system. If you have lost any SKILL points, all but 1 are restored. Cautiously, you move on, coming to Silver Street. Turn to **85**.

176

The vile monstrosity sinks to the ground, squelching in a pool of blood and green ichor. The stench of its spilled entrails is nauseating. The sages are woebegone at the death of their creation, but they help you out of the pit. 'I'm sorry,' says Moreau, 'my spell did not work. What a shame you had to kill her.' You shake your head at their madness and ask for your gold. Polonius dives his hands into various pockets and folds of his robes, a look of consternation crossing his features. He is about to make some excuse, when he sees your growing anger. Eventually, he offers you a magic scroll as payment instead. It contains a Spell of Agonizing Doom, which you can use once only. You accept, take your leave, and head for the house of the Sage. Turn to **273**.

177

You charge at the Druid, your sword raised. Before you can strike, your jaw drops in amazement. Where once there was a man carrying an oak staff, there is now a skylark. Trilling shrilly, it flies around you and away. After a few minutes you see the skylark wheeling above you again. It could be trying to draw attention to you, or perhaps it is preparing to attack you itself. If you leave the clearing, turn to **187**. If you wish to stay and hide, turn to **147**.

178

The Dragon says, 'You must believe me. If you do not, you will die trying the portal, and I cannot carry the Talisman through.' Its honey-smooth voice beguiles you with its gentle charm. *Test your Luck*. If you are Lucky, turn to **129**. If you are Unlucky, turn to **118**.

179
You hastily hand the Talisman to the skeletal envoy of Death. As he receives it, he seems to draw unholy strength from it. 'You fool,' he mocks, his voice deep and resonant, full of malice. He touches you with the Talisman uncannily quickly. It is as if Death himself had touched you and your heart beats no more. Nothing can save you. Your quest ends here.

180
You run down the stairs four at a time. You reach another landing before you hear the tramp of feet coming up from below. Thinking quickly, you hide behind an arras. *Test your Luck*. If you are Lucky, turn to **140**. If you are Unlucky, turn to **153**.

181

The cut-throat yields and you are looked at with some admiration and respect. The barman tries to make light of things saying, 'You are truly a mighty warrior – you could even be a match for Tyutchev.' He tells you the story of Heimdol the Mighty. It seems that Heimdol was one of the strongest and most unpleasant men ever to swill ale at the Red Dragon. One day a stranger, Tyutchev, accepted his challenge to a bout of arm-wrestling. Heimdol lost for the first time in his life. He was furious and threatened awful reprisals if Tyutchev ever returned. A few nights later Tyutchev did return and began to insult Heimdol and two of his friends. In the inevitable fight which followed, Tyutchev killed them all and carved his initials on Heimdol's forehead. 'He worships the God of insane chaos, Anarchil, and since that night none has dared gainsay him here.' If you want to ask the whereabouts of the Thieves' Guild, turn to **210**. If you would rather ask the cut-throats for aid in completing some unfinished business, turn to **223**.

'We are scholars,' says Moreau excitedly. 'Vivisection is our field of study. We use surgery and magic to create new forms of life. Just wait till you see our creation.' They take you to a large sunken pit in the middle of the massive greenhouse. The pit is ringed at the top with downward pointing spikes. They lower a ladder and you all descend into it. In a barred cage at the edge of the pit is a most loathsome sight. The scholars' creation is a massive beast with the body of a giant cockroach, six giant arms for legs and two heads, one above the other. The top one is the head of a crocodile and below is the warty face of an ogre. 'Isn't she beautiful?' says Moreau. Polonius says, 'We need a valiant warrior to test her. We want her to be used as a war-beast. Do not worry, though; the minute she looks like harming you, Polonius here will put her to sleep with a special spell.' The ogre face, which looks distinctly male, roars and slavers. If you want to say, 'Thank you, no, I'm not fighting that,' and leave immediately, turn to **201**. If you would rather say, 'This should be interesting,' and prepare to fight the beast, turn to **189**.

183

You turn right, down Trader's Row, and walk for some way, looking for the storm-drain. Eventually you see it and, checking that you are unobserved, jump down it. You land up to your ankles in slime. You wade down the huge drain until you come to a small round door set in the left-hand wall. *Test your Luck*. If you are Lucky, turn to **238**. If you are Unlucky, turn to **205**.

184

An inscription on the circular pillar reads:

*Behind the symbol on the first door
lies that which you risk your life for.*

As you try to work out the meaning of this strange message, a pool of water forms around your feet. You look up just as a crack splits the ceiling. A torrent of water pours down. You jump forward as, with a grating rumble, a slab of rock starts to fall from the roof across the exit ahead. Your only hope is to throw yourself through the narrowing gap. Roll two dice. If the total is equal to or less than your SKILL score, turn to **103**. If the result is greater than your SKILL score, turn to **215**.

185

Suddenly, you are in blinding sunshine. You are standing at the lip of an immense chasm. You realize that this must be the Rift the Crusaders spoke of. The rocky earth is blackened and cracked, full of pits and fissures, and noisome fumes rise from the depths of the chasm. To the west you see a range of green hills partially covered in trees and thick woodland. A few hundred metres to your right you can see where a forest begins, extending all the way to the hills. You realize that you must head in the direction of the hills to reach Greyguilds – but which route will you take? If you go through the forest, turn to **256**. If you would rather take the more direct route across open ground, turn to **134**.

186

You leave the building and continue on down Booker's Walk. The streets are already deserted and there are few lights in this part of the city. You search for the welcoming light of an inn. Then, without warning, the steel teeth of a hidden man-trap snap shut round your leg, ripping your flesh. You are in terrible pain. Lose 2 STAMINA points. Shadowy figures loom out of the murk all around you. Their faces glow with a sickly pallor in the moonlight. They are wearing black robes clasped at the neck by shrunken human skulls. Do you still have the Talisman of Death? If you have, turn to **162**. If you have not got it, turn to **150**.

187

You leave the clearing, anxious that you should not anger the Druid further by staying in the Sacred Grove. Turn to **159**.

188

You run for the door to the street at the back of the church. Somnus sees you and points majestically. 'Die,' he whispers. A huge dark figure appears before you, a great black sword in its hand. It has black wings of shadow and a tall white crest sweeps back from the black helmet which hides its features. Your heart palpitates wildly and then stops beating. The mere sight of the ANGEL OF DEATH destroys you. You will wander the barren plain of the Valley of Death until the end of time.

189

'Excellent, excellent,' enthuses Moreau. They climb the ladder and draw it up behind them. With a clang the bars of the cage slide into the ground. The beast comes towards you, intent on making you its next meal. You must fight the VIVISECT. The Sages produce wax tablets and begin to take notes.

VIVISECT   SKILL 8   STAMINA 12

You may appeal for help at any time. If you do, remember this reference number and turn to **158**. If you do not appeal and win, turn to **176**.

190

When you have laid your weapons aside, the Dragon beckons you to the portal. When you get close it says, 'You man-things are so easily tricked.' It jumps upon you and rends you limb from limb. Turn to **43**.

191

The Captain nods and says, 'We will escort you safely to Greyguilds. These moors are well known for brigands. Perhaps you would like to ride behind Elvira here.' She points to one of the younger women. You thank her and accept a helping hand up, thankful to rest your legs. Elvira does not seem too pleased at having to share her horse with you and you ride across the wilderness in silence. Turn to **268**.

192

At last you reach the floor of the plateau itself. It seems your aching legs have forgotten how to walk on level ground. The vegetation is lush, like a tropical rain forest, and your clothes cling to you, damp with perspiration. As you pause to listen to the screech of a scarlet macaw a group of HOGMEN burst from the vegetation in front of you. They are blue-grey, hairy and have heads like tusked boars. Will you tell them that you mean no harm (turn to **151**), or attack them (turn to **172**)?

193

You are weakening. You realize you are close to death. A sudden blinding light halts the Death-knight's onslaught. To your amazement the Paladin crusader stands before you, bathed in a silvery radiance. The Death-knight steps back, shielding its face. The Paladins' Holy Sword hums through the air and cuts the Death-knight in two. As abruptly as he came, the Paladin disappears. There is no sign of your adversary but the Holy Sword remains, casting a glow where it lies on the straw. You pick it up, realizing that it is meant for you to use in your struggle against Death. As you grasp it, your wounds heal magically. You regain 6 STAMINA points. You may add 1 to your SKILL when using the Holy Sword. Turn to 121.

194

You drive your sword into his back. He lets out a scream of pain as he dies. Lord Min, a small, agile young man is behind you. He says, 'Sloppily done. We may all pay for that. Now, hurry!' Turn to 283.

195

You continue along Cobbler's Walk, turning a corner or two. Suddenly, a body comes crashing through a nearby window into the street. Splinters of glass fly everywhere, but you are unharmed. Moving closer you see the mangled corpse of a man dressed in black robes covered with odd symbols. A door to the nearby house bursts open and a man dressed in a silver robe with black symbols, runs into the street screaming, 'Flee! Run for your life!' as he disappears. In the open doorway a monstrous figure now stands. It springs at you with a demonic howl. It is three metres high, with the head and hind legs of an elk. Its bloated humanoid torso is mottled blue and grey and its breath clouds the air with crystals of ice. It points at you and a gale of freezing sleet hits you. The chill is almost crippling – lose 3 STAMINA points. If you are still alive, the Demon reaches for you with its powerful talons. You must fight it.

ICE DEMON   SKILL 8   STAMINA 10

If you win, turn to **61**.

The Sage shows you to a side room, full of reading desks. A few are occupied by students of history, young and old. With an expansive gesture he points to a wall lined with shelves, which are filled with scrolls and tablets. You choose a set of scrolls called *Greyguilds Revisited*, by Nyleve. It is the story of a dissolute young nobleman who failed to take advantage of the education offered by the Guilds of Learning. You are able to glean much interesting information about the city. The religious orders hold all the power. You are astonished to find that Vagar, the God of thieves, liars and cut-throats, has most followers within the city. There is a temple to Death in the city as well. Indeed it seems that Greyguilds is not the tranquil city that it once was. The armed forces protecting the city come from two groups, the warrior-women who worship the evil goddess Fell-Kyrinla, and the followers of the All-Mother. Greyguilds lies on the edge of a large plain, called the Manmarch, or lands of men. It is just one of many cities in this part of the world. As you are wondering whether you will ever visit Doomover, or the Spires of Foreshadowing, the other students begin filing out. With a start you realize it is already dark and you leave quickly, looking for a safe place to sleep. Turn to **186**.

197

Suddenly, from behind you, the Captain shouts, 'Look out! Ambush! Everybody duck!' You hear the sound of an arrow whistling through the air as Elvira ducks in front of you. Will you duck (turn to **240**) or wait to see what happens (turn to **224**)?

198

'You have come across the wilderness? Did you by any chance come across a man dressed in green robes similar to my own? He would have carried an oak staff and worn a crown of mistletoe; he would have told you his name.' Will you answer:

'I did not meet him'?	Turn to **226**
'His name was Dwithian'?	Turn to **212**
'His name was Wodeman'?	Turn to **166**

199

As you are looking around you, checking that there is no mate near by to avenge her death, a green-robed figure appears in the centre of the clearing, as if by magic. He has an oak staff in one hand and a silver sickle in the other. A crown of mistletoe rests on his head. Striking the ground with his staff, he says, 'I am the Guardian Druid of this Sacred Grove and you have slain my friend, Snowmane, and left her cubs motherless. May the hand that killed her never be still.' You feel a tremor running down your arm – your sword-hand begins to shake. Lose 1 SKILL point for the Druid's curse. If you attack the Druid in order to force him to lift the curse, turn to **177**. If you decide not to risk further dealings with this man and leave the clearing, turn to **159**.

During the fight the brass tiger charm falls to the floor. Now that it is gone you realize that it was cursed and that it forced you to insult the barman. You make no attempt to recover it. The cut-throat yields and you are looked at with some admiration and respect. The barman tries to make light of things saying, 'You are truly a mighty warrior – you could even be a match for Tyutchev.' He tells you the story of how Tyutchev beat Heimdol the Mighty. It seems that Heimdol was one of the strongest and most unpleasant men ever to swill ale at the Red Dragon. One day a stranger, Tyutchev, accepted his challenge to a bout of arm-wrestling. Heimdol lost for the first time in his life. He was furious and threatened awful reprisals if Tyutchev ever returned. A few nights later Tyutchev did return and began to insult Heimdol and two of his friends. In the inevitable fight which followed, Tyutchev killed them all and carved his initials on Heimdol's forehead. 'He worships the God of insane chaos, Anarchil, and since that night none has dared gainsay him here.' If you want to ask the whereabouts of the Thieves' Guild, turn to **236**. If you would rather ask them for aid in completing some unfinished business, turn to **246**.

201

'Ah well, that's a pity,' says Polonius, and presses the far wall of the pit. With a great clang bars spring up between you and the two scholars. To your horror you see that at the same time the bars separating you from their awful creation have slid into the ground. The beast comes towards you, intent on turning you into a meal. You must fight the VIVISECT. The scholars produce wax tablets and begin to take notes.

VIVISECT   SKILL 8   STAMINA 12

You may appeal for help at any time. If you do, remember this reference number and turn to **158**. If you do not appeal, and win, turn to **176**.

202

The guard beckons you inside the temple. Just as you enter you almost bump into Hawkana, the tall, raven-haired High Priestess. 'Who is this?' she barks. The guard explains that you claim to be a secret messenger, but have failed to give any password. Hawkana says, 'This person is no messenger. Die, desecrator!' Cursing your ill luck at meeting Hawkana so soon after entering the temple, you turn to run. Hawkana lets out a scream of invocation, calling on the powers of her Goddess. A pillar of flame engulfs you as the power of Fell-Kyrinla is unleashed. You are burnt to a cinder. Turn to **109**.

203

When you reach the floor of the valley, you find a pool into which a spring is bubbling. Feeling thirsty after having come so far, you step forward to the pool to drink where the branches of a gnarled old willow meet the water. Almost immediately you begin to feel strangely sleepy and realize that you are swaying, about to topple into the pool. *Test your Luck.* If you are Lucky, turn to **36**. If you are Unlucky, turn to **319**.

204

Just as you approach a door ahead, you hear a crack and the sound of rushing water behind you. A slab of rock is slithering down, slowly blocking the exit from the room you have just left. It suddenly slams to the floor with a crash, before much of the water that is filling the room can flow into the tunnel towards you. You can only go on. Turn to **120**.

205

As you are about to open the door, you hear a click and something thumps you on the back. Looking down you see the bloody head of a harpoon protruding from your stomach. Your hands clutch at the gaping wound as you try to stop your entrails spilling into the slime of the sewer. Mercifully, death takes you swiftly. Turn to **109**.

206

You strike the old temple-servant across the back of his neck with the pommel of your sword. He collapses soundlessly. You go to tie him up. 'Good work,' says Lord Min, a small, agile young man. 'Now I'll finish it.' He steps forward with his dagger, meaning to slit the old man's throat. Will you stop him (turn to **251**), or let him kill the old man (turn to **239**)?

207

Your pitch-soaked torch flares brightly. The WRAITH reins its hell-steed in before you. It carries an aura of fear but you stare defiantly into the black emptiness of its face. It hisses with frustration and, in a voice hoarse with age, says, 'Death will take what is his and you shall become one of us. For we shall return with our full strength – we are the instruments of Death.' It turns its nightmarish steed and disappears into the night. Your rest thereafter is troubled and you regain only 1 STAMINA point. Turn to **154**.

208

The footsteps come on and from the air above you a dull rasping voice intones: 'I am a spirit of the dead and we are beyond number.' Suddenly a terrible blow knocks you backwards. Lose 2 STAMINA points. You must fight the UNSEEN STALKER, striking out blindly and hoping your thrusts will harm it.

UNSEEN STALKER   SKILL 9   STAMINA 8

If you win, turn to **250**.

209

Scarface looks you up and down for a moment. Then he says, 'Right, I'll get the Guildmaster, we'll see what he has to say.' There is an uneasy silence before he returns with another man. Scarface says, 'This is Vagrant, Guildmaster of Thieves.' Vagrant is a handsome, middle-aged man wearing an ermine jacket. Twirling his moustache, he asks you the purpose of your visit. What will you say:

You need help to steal something?	Turn to **315**
You want to steal the Talisman of Death?	Turn to **276**
You will lead them to a hoard of priceless jewellery?	Turn to **291**

210

Your request comes out more like a demand, spoken tersely and loudly. Nevertheless, one of them tells you that the entrance to the Thieves' Guild is through an open storm-drain which leads into the sewers near Trader's Row. You gruffly tell them to meet you there at midday tomorrow. You decide to leave straight away, before you insult anyone else. On your way to the door the gloom darkens as two people come down the steps from the street. The first has to stoop to avoid hitting his head. His tall wiry frame is wreathed in a cloak that seems to deepen the darkness about him. The only hint of colour is his hair, very curly and dyed bright corn-yellow. The second is a handsome young woman, dressed in a bizarre patchwork of armour. 'Tyutchev, Cassandra, welcome!' cries the barman obsequiously. They wait for you to step out of their way. 'Get out of my way, Orc breath,' you say before you can stop yourself. With a flash of insight you realize the brass tiger charm must be cursed. Tyutchev smiles. They step to either side of you, drawing their swords. Together they strike with the speed and grace of panthers. Tyutchev's sword is almost as tall as you are and he wields it negligently in one hand. Cassandra's glows coldly. Every time she hits you, subtract 3 STAMINA points.

	SKILL	STAMINA
TYUTCHEV	10	12
CASSANDRA	9	10

If you reduce Cassandra's STAMINA to 4 or less she drops back and Tyutchev moves in to cover her. If you reduce Tyutchev's STAMINA to 4 or less, turn to **355**.

211

The Dragon says, 'This is a grave matter indeed. The Talisman must go through the portal. I will tell you something: I cannot pass through the portal. As you can see, it is too small for my bulk. You can pass through, but only if you leave behind any metal you are carrying. The gods have set a powerful magic to stop weapons being brought through from the other side. I will let you pass but, for your own sake you must do as I suggest.' Will you lay down any weapons and money before stepping through (turn to **190**), or ask him if he takes you for a fool (turn to **178**)?

212

'I see,' she says shortly and turns away. She walks off and is soon lost in the crowd. You shrug your shoulders and walk on. Turn to **130**.

213

You run back into the room with the skylight, but there is nothing to be seen. The rope is gone and the skylight is shut. You hear the tramp of feet coming up the stairs. You look around desperately but there is nowhere to hide. Ten of the warrior-women burst in. You fight valiantly but there are too many of them. You are overwhelmed and slain. Turn to **109**.

214

As you close with the Elves, one of them makes a strange gesture. You realize with horror that he is using magic. A drowsy paralysis seizes your limbs and you are unable to move. Laughing cruelly, they bind you hand and foot. You are to be taken down into the Rift and you will never see daylight again. Your quest ends here.

215

Too late. The descending rock traps you and your ribcage collapses like a concertina. Turn to **43**.

216

The boy leads you to the Guilds of Learning. You hurry down a cloister, which surrounds a square of tall grass speckled with scarlet poppies, and on towards a huge greenhouse made of tarred wood and glass. Two scholars wearing the pale blue robes of the Sages come out to greet you. One is spindly and bald, the other is very chubby and peers at you through his pince-nez. They are obviously pleased to see you and introduce themselves as Moreau and Polonius. The fat one, Polonius, asks you to come with them, if you would like to earn twenty gold pieces for twenty minutes' work. Will you go with them into the greenhouse (turn to **182**), or politely decline and go back to the Sage's house (turn to **273**)?

217

You creep up behind the old man as he shuffles along the corridor. Will you use the pommel of your sword and try to knock him out (turn to **206**), or strike him down with your sword (turn to **194**)?

218

Hastily, you leave the clearing. Luckily, it seems she was interested only in protecting her cubs. You press on through the wood towards the hills, skirting the clearing. Turn to **159**.

219

As you run through the darkness the Talisman grows heavier, weighing you down. You cannot keep ahead of your pursuer. A flaming hoof strikes you down. Lose 2 STAMINA points. If you are still alive, you must fight this monstrous WRAITH. Whenever it hits you, you feel a cold, numbing sensation as it drains your life-force. Lose 1 SKILL point each time it strikes you.

WRAITH   SKILL 9   STAMINA 10

If you win, turn to **174**.

'Lies,' it hisses, and lunges at you with its rapier before you can move. A chill numbness spreads from the wound and you feel as if your life-blood is being drained away. Lose 1 SKILL and 2 STAMINA points. Now you must fight the ENVOY OF DEATH. Each time it strikes you, you must lose 1 SKILL point as well as the normal STAMINA loss.

ENVOY OF DEATH	SKILL 8	STAMINA 6

If you win, turn to **254**.

221

You spot one of the warrior-women who you know are members of the temple of Fell-Kyrinla. Hoping she is on her way to the temple, you follow her at a distance. Eventually, you come to a building made of a white stone, with dark grey columns. Steps lead up to the entrance between two pillars and there is a guard at the top. What will you do:

Attack the guard?   Turn to **234**
Tell her you have a message for the
   High Priestess?   Turn to **202**
Give up and go to the Red Dragon
   Inn   Turn to **24**

'How dare you desecrate the temple. How dare you interrupt me when I'm speaking with the Goddess,' she says softly, white with rage. 'I dedicate your soul to the Goddess.' She drives her fist into the air and chops it downwards. A pillar of flame descends from the vaulted roof. Roll one die. If you score 1–4, turn to **105**. If you score a 5 or a 6, turn to **132**.

They appear interested and offer you some ale. You accept a mug and do not drink. You suggest that in helping you they might gain a great deal. They agree to meet you and tell you to come to the Thieves' Guild at midday tomorrow, via the disguised coal-hole in Hornbeam Road. You are beginning to chat to them when two newcomers enter the ale cellar. 'Ah! Tyutchev, Cassandra, welcome!' cries the barman obsequiously. The thieves with whom you are sitting move quickly to another table. The first stranger is a very tall, wiry, man whose frame is wreathed in a black cloak which seems to deepen the darkness around him. The only hint of colour is his hair, very curly and dyed bright corn-yellow. The second is a handsome young woman dressed in a bizarre patchwork of armour. The man, Tyutchev, strolls to the bar, but the woman called Cassandra comes over and sits at your table, looking you over. 'Find your own table, wrinkled hag,' you say before you can stop yourself. With a flash of insight you realize that the brass tiger charm must be cursed. Cassandra spits in your face and moving with the grace of a panther, draws her sword. It glows coldly and is rimed with frost. Each time she attacks successfully you lose 3 STAMINA points as biting cold sears your wound. Tyutchev merely looks on, grinning.

CASSANDRA   SKILL 9   STAMINA 10

If you reduce Cassandra's STAMINA to 4 or less turn to **342**.

224

Realizing that the whole thing was a trick designed to test you, you make no move and the arrow, fired by one of the women, thuds harmlessly into a tree. They now believe that you are truly deaf and dumb. You ride on into the late afternoon, moving from the wilderness to a grey and desolate moor. Ahead you can see the walls of a large city. A salute is given as you approach the huge arched gate in the fortified wall. The Captain gestures to you to dismount and waves you into Greyguilds itself. Thankful for your escort, you wave farewell and set out to discover if there is any way of returning to Earth. Turn to **296**.

225

The fireball erupts around you. The excruciating pain and the smell of your burnt flesh tells you that it was real. Lose 6 STAMINA points. If you are still alive, you hear Thaum laughing cruelly as Tyutchev moves to attack. Turn to **265**.

226

'Ah, it is a long time since we had news. I am a Priestess of the All-Mother, the Fountain of Life. The Druids are our friends. I trust you will enjoy your stay in Greyguilds. Goodbye, stranger.' She walks on and is soon lost in the crowd. You continue on down Store Street. Turn to **130**.

227

Your legs are beginning to grow heavy as you reach a gap between two hills. You are slowing now, and wonder how much longer you can keep this up. Looking back, you are pleased to see that the Elves and Orcs have met and are engaged in bloody battle. The Elves are making short work of the Orcs – strange sparks leap from their hands, killing the Orcs instantly. You realize that any respite you have gained will be short-lived, and press on. Over the hill you come to a verdant valley, deep in ferns. Turn to **203**.

228

You hurry on down the stairs but the old man has seen you. Turn to **283**.

229

On your way towards the Sage's house a small boy runs up to you and asks if you would like to help a very clever scholar and make some money doing it. 'It won't take long,' he adds, tugging at your sleeve. Do you want to thank him, but decline and go on your way (turn to **273**), or will you go with the boy (turn to **216**)?

230

You wade carefully into the scum-covered pond and hold out your hand to the old woman. There is a sudden churning in the water and slimy tentacles slither around your thighs. The old woman's head rears up at you, revealing a huge, horny beak where her chest should have been, above a bloated body, sprouting six tentacles. You must fight the GRENDEL.

GRENDEL   SKILL 8   STAMINA 9

If you win, turn to **65**.

231

Instead of plummeting right down to the plateau, the magical Roc's feather holds you up and you drift gently down to land on the steps seventeen metres below. You start to climb up again, keeping a careful look out. Turn to **192**.

232

Drawing your sword, you run forward to attack.

WHITE
SHE-WOLF   SKILL 8   STAMINA 9

If you win, turn to **199**.

233

The alchemist gives you the Vial of Vapours of Speed in exchange for the gold, telling you to inhale the Vapours when you wish to speed up your actions. If you have any money left, you can buy any of his other wares which you haven't tried:

Barkskin – 7 gold pieces.	Turn to **306**
Fortunate Luckstone – 10 gold pieces.	Turn to **266**
Elixir of Life – 12 gold pieces.	Turn to **360**
Or are you ready to leave and continue on your way?	Turn to **28**

234

As you rush up the stairs, the guard strikes a hidden bell and attacks you. You must fight her.

TEMPLE GUARD   SKILL 6   STAMINA 8

If you win turn to **255**.

235

As you catch your breath three shadows appear on the road before you. Looking up, you see Tyutchev and Cassandra, with a hideous squid-like creature hovering in the air between them. One of the squid's tentacles is curled loosely around Cassandra's waist. 'We meet again,' says Tyutchev. 'Young Lord Min tells me you have been successful. Congratulations, you have done us a favour. Now you'll be glad your peril is over. We are taking the Talisman.' Grimly, you draw your sword. 'I see,' says Tyutchev. 'Then let me introduce Thaum,' he continues, gesturing towards the squid-like monster. Its form dissolves and becomes the man with the gold ear-ring and flowing grey robes you saw producing flowers out of the air for the crowds. He is a Master of Illusion. At that moment a huge and ugly Troll appears from within the safe house. 'Here is Harg,' says Thaum. Harg raises a huge hammer ready to strike you. Is he real, or is he one of Thaum's illusions? If you attack the Troll, turn to **45**. If you allow his hammer to strike you, turn to **141**.

236

They invite you to join them for a drink, which you do. One of them tells you that the entrance to the Thieves' Guild is through an open storm-drain which leads into the sewers near Trader's Row. They will meet you there at midday tomorrow. Turn to **169**.

237

Coming along Moorgate you realize that the guards on the gate have been doubled, following the death of Hawkana. To your dismay, a mounted patrol enters Moorgate from Smith Street and you are trapped between the cavalry and the guards at the gate. As you slip through the gate, one of the warrior-women recognizes you. They scream for your blood. You flee across the wilderness, but the cavalry are swifter and there is nowhere to hide. You turn and fight, but there are too many of them and they are hungry for revenge. The end is mercifully swift. Turn to **109**.

238

As you open the door you slip on the slime underfoot. A glancing blow catches you on the side as a harpoon thuds into the door. Lose 2 STAMINA points. If you are still alive, you look behind and see the firing mechanism of the trap. You open the door and step into a magnificently furnished room. Evidently the Thieves' Guild lacks nothing. A group of men, some of whom you recognize from the Red Dragon, are lounging on sofas. They leap to their feet in surprise and reach for their swords. Will you place your back to the wall and draw your sword (turn to **242**), or calmly tell them that you have been invited (turn to **252**)?

239

The old man gurgles softly and dies. Lord Min grins wolfishly. Lose 1 LUCK point for your callous action. You hurry on down the stairs which lead to a set of double doors. A guard is on duty but she is over-whelmed before she can make a sound. Inside the Inner Sanctum of the temple a tall raven-haired woman is praying at the altar, upon which lies the Talisman of Death. She appears to be talking to her goddess, Fell-Kyrinla. Beyond the altar is a large marble statue of the goddess, wearing chainmail, her expression arrogant and cruelly beautiful. The tall woman rises and turns towards you. 'Hounds of Hell! It's Hawkana, the High Priestess!' breathes Jemmy the Rat. 'I'm off.' You look around to see the thieves have disappeared. Before you can try to follow, Hawkana casts a spell and the doors fly shut. Turn to **222**.

240

You duck and hear the sound of an arrow embed-ding itself in a tree some way off. 'Oh ho!' you hear the Captain crow. 'Suddenly regained our sense of hearing, have we? A truly miraculous recovery.' She shouts a command and Elvira twists in the saddle and throws you to the ground. Landing on top of you, she knocks the breath out of you and overpowers you. Your hands are tied behind your back and your sword is taken. From now on you must fight with your dagger. Lose 2 SKILL points. When you acquire another sword you may restore them. Turn to **257**.

241

Scarface leads you through a maze of back alleys into a building that Jemmy the Rat tells you is a safe house. You climb on to the roof and continue running across the roof-tops of the city. Soon you are on top of a tall house, just below the top of the temple to Fell-Kyrinla. Bloodheart, a hulking, silent fellow, takes a rope and grappling hook from his shoulder. He effortlessly throws it round the top of one of the temple columns. He secures his end to a chimney-stack and walks across on the tightrope he has created. You all manage to cross hand-over-hand and join him in the temple eaves. Jemmy the Rat, a wiry man with fingers like spider's legs, finds a skylight and, true to his name, prises off the bars and picks the lock. Reaching inside he disarms a trap containing a poisoned dart. You marvel at his nimble-fingered skill. They lower a rope and you all drop down to the top of a staircase. You catch sight of an old serving-man passing a doorway on the landing. The others have not noticed him. Will you silence him, in case he has seen you (turn to **217**), or ignore him, hoping he didn't see you (turn to **228**)?

242

As they move towards you, one of them produces a crossbow and fires. You duck but he was aiming at your leg and the bolt slams into your thigh, spinning you sideways. You feel as if your veins are on fire. The bolt was poisoned, and you soon sink into the oblivion of death. Turn to **109**.

243

You continue along Store Street and then down a tree-lined avenue called Booker's Walk. Two very grand buildings, built of blocks of grey stone, stand on either side of the road. A group of young people in blue togas, escorted by a white-haired old man in pale blue robes, enters the building opposite. A flag, showing books and scrolls, is flying from the nearest building; it appears to be a library. Will you see what information the library has to offer (turn to **346**), or investigate the other building, to find out what the young people are doing (turn to **279**)?

244

The fireball bursts behind you, but a burning pain sears your back and you smell charred cloth. Lose 3 STAMINA points. If you are still alive, you press home your attack on Tyutchev. Turn to **265**.

Just as you are about to enter the bare, roofless room, a rotten stair breaks, betraying your presence. Realizing that they may have been overheard, one of the thieves runs off across a nearby roof-top. The other two, mean-looking thugs in brown breeches, attack you. They try to come at you from different sides, but after springing up the last stairs your footwork is too good for them and you hold the stairway, where they can only come at you one at a time. You must fight them in order.

	SKILL	STAMINA
First THIEF	6	7
Second THIEF	7	6

If you win, turn to **329**.

246

They appear interested and offer you some ale. You accept a mug and do not drink. You suggest that in helping you, they might gain a great deal. They agree to meet you and tell you to come to the Thieves' Guild at midday tomorrow, via the disguised coal-hole in Hornbeam Road. You begin to chat to them. Turn to **169**.

247

Her eyebrows rise in surprise. All four of them look at you in disbelief. The man in gold turns to the Priest in the white surcoat and asks, 'Is it the truth?' Knowing your story to be true, you decide to wait while the Priest casts a spell. 'It is the truth,' he says, 'and spoken from a true heart.' The Shieldmaiden lowers the bow and moves over to guard the entrance of the cavern. 'What are we to do? The exits are blocked and I have only the power to teleport one of us out now,' says the man in gold. 'Perhaps this warrior has been sent by the gods to continue the quest.' Sensing the goodness in these people, you wait to hear how you can aid them. Turn to **100**.

248

You are swept up in the talons of a great white eagle. Your assailants are soon specks below you on the street. Rising high above the roof-tops you look to the south-east and see, far away, a mountain on top of a large plateau. A voice speaks in your head – the voice of the All-Mother. 'That is Mount Star-reach, your goal. At its summit lies the portal that will take you back to your own world.' For a moment it seems the eagle will bear you to the mountain, but the Talisman seems to weigh like a ball of lead around your neck and the eagle is forced to land in a deserted alley of Store Street. Before you can thank it, it takes to the air again and is soon soaring far above the city. Are you wearing magical chainmail? If you are, turn to **375**. If not, turn to **258**.

249

You hurry along to the Moorgate itself. There is a group of warriors on guard, men and women, in green livery. They are followers of the All-Mother who have been given your description by Lillantha. They wave you through the gate and you walk out into the night. Gain 1 LUCK point for escaping the city. Turn to **8**.

250

Exhausted from the rigours of the day, you stop and draw breath. The attack by an unseen foe has left you unnerved. You look around, then listen carefully in case another attack should be imminent. As night falls you are thankful to find an empty stable. You go in and curl up in a heap of straw, ready for the night. Turn to **91**.

251

You reach out and knock the young thief's hand away. He drops his dagger, which clatters noisily all the way down the stairs. 'Sentimental fool!' he snaps. 'The guards will have heard that.' He draws another dagger from his boot. 'Hurry, we have little time now,' says Scarface. You hurry on. Turn to **283**.

252

'If we had really wanted you to come, don't you think we would have told you the safe route?' says a thief with a scar running from ear to chin, whom you recognize from the Red Dragon. They move towards you purposefully. 'This is the welcome we give to the likes of you,' he continues. Will you place your back to the wall and draw your sword (turn to 242), or sit down, telling them to kill you if they like, but they'll miss out on an attractive proposition (turn to 209)?

253

The river winds between the hills. You wade along it, knowing that the Dark Elves will lose your scent in the water. After a while, you climb out on the other side of the river and continue on your way. Turn to 331.

Your last blow meets no resistance. The skeletal form collapses to the ground in a heap. All is silent except for a sudden keening of the wind. You rest and begin to overcome the shock to your system. If you have lost any SKILL points, all except 1 are restored. Cautiously, you continue along Store Street and then down a tree-lined avenue called Booker's Walk. Two very grand buildings, built of blocks of grey stone, stand on either side of the road. A group of young people in blue togas, escorted by a white-haired old man in pale blue robes, enters the building opposite. A flag showing books and scrolls is flying from the nearest building; it appears to be a library. Will you see what information the library has to offer (turn to 346), or investigate the other building, to find out what the young people are doing (turn to 279)?

255

As the stricken woman slides down the temple steps, leaving a trail of blood behind her, you are dismayed to see Hawkana, the raven-haired High Priestess. She lets out a scream of invocation, calling on the powers of her Goddess. A pillar of flame engulfs you as the power of Fell-Kyrinla is unleashed. You are burnt to a cinder. Turn to **109**.

256

You enter the green, gloomy shade of the woods. After a while, you stumble into a clearing and stop in surprise at the sight that greets you. A huge, white SHE-WOLF, almost as large as a pony, is suckling two cubs. She pushes them aside and crouches, snarling. Will you:

Back off and leave?	Turn to **218**
Offer the wolf some dried meat?	Turn to **52**
Attack her?	Turn to **232**

257

You ride on into the late afternoon, moving from the wilderness to a grey and desolate moor. Ahead you can see the walls of a large city. A salute is given as you approach the huge arched gate in the fortified wall. The Captain details half her patrol to remain on guard at the gate. Turning to you she says, 'We are taking you to Hawkana – she will want to ask you some questions.' Do you want to seize the first opportunity to fight your way out (turn to **318**), or go quietly and see what happens (turn to **334**)?

258

Store Street is an extension of Moorgate. Will you hurry down Store Street to the end of Moorgate (turn to **237**), or, if you had dinner with a Sage, ask the way to the cemetery (turn to **261**)?

259

The cut-throats yield. 'It seems you are a match for us, warrior,' says Scarface. The thieves look at you with admiration and respect. Will you demand that they tell you how to get to the Thieves' Guild (turn to **236**), or say you have some unfinished business they might like to help you with (turn to **246**)?

260

You walk down the tunnel which turns left again. As you round the corner you hear an ominous sound from the room you have just left. You dart back to see the ceiling crashing down, a set of vicious spikes protruding from it. A slab of rock is sliding down, gradually blocking the entrance. It slams to the floor with a crash and then all is quiet. You can only go on. Turn to **120**.

261

You stop a passing student who directs you to the cemetery. You run down Pallbearer's Row, anxious to escape from the city. As you approach the cemetery, an ox-cart, returning from the market, loses a wheel and overturns, almost blocking the road. You run for the gap between it and the cemetery wall, but it is blocked by a man with a shaven head. He wears baggy scarlet trousers which end just below the knee and a loose scarlet jacket tied with a black cotton belt. On his forehead is a tattoo of a scarlet praying mantis. He doesn't seem inclined to let you pass. Will you:

Ask him politely to let you through?	Turn to **338**
Tell him to get out of your way?	Turn to **311**
Attack him?	Turn to **288**

262

As you open the book, the scales glitter and seem to change colour. Its title is *Tome of Misfortune* and the letters on the page seem to glow ominously. You shut the book, but it is too late. You can feel the malice of evil magic. You are the victim of some ancient curse! Lose 1 LUCK point. You leave the Guilds of Learning in disgust. Turn to **186**.

263

You fall all the way down the cliff-face, bouncing a few times against the rock. You are dead long before you land at the base of a violet creeper. Turn to **43**.

264

As dusk comes, you walk on down the Street of Seven Sins until you reach the Red Dragon Inn. A thick-set man opens the door and flings a pail of red, stained sawdust across the road. 'Sorry, closed,' he growls at you and slams the door again. Before you can move you notice the pile of sawdust being disturbed. Footsteps appear, one by one, leading from the sawdust towards you. Will you:

Shout loudly, to attract attention?	Turn to **297**
Scoop up some dirt and fling it at the footsteps?	Turn to **348**
Wait to see what happens?	Turn to **208**

265

Tyutchev's bastard sword, almost as long as you, hums through the air as he parries your first attack with the agility of a cat. The black cloak he wears makes it difficult for you to tell exactly where he is. Cassandra and Thaum, looking confident, stand back to watch. You fight Tyutchev.

TYUTCHEV   SKILL 10   STAMINA 12

After your first successful attack on him, turn to **301**.

266

The alchemist gives you the Fortunate Luckstone in exchange for the gold. You can feel its power when he hands it to you. Add 1 to your LUCK score. If you have not tried them already, you can buy any of his other wares:

Barkskin – 7 gold pieces.   Turn to **306**
Vapours of Speed – 10 gold pieces.   Turn to **233**
Elixir of Life – 12 gold pieces.   Turn to **360**
Or are you ready to leave and
    continue on your way?   Turn to **28**

267

Creeping stealthily, you barely rustle the dried leaves underfoot. The soporific BASILISK does not even notice you, which is just as well. Its eyes flicker open for a moment and a small mouse which happens to be running across its line of vision slows and turns to stone. You hurry quickly on your way, lest you suffer the same fate. Turn to **270**.

268

You ride on into the late afternoon, moving from the wilderness to a grey and desolate moor. Ahead you can see the walls of a large city. A salute is given as you approach the huge arched gate in the fortified wall. The Captain tells you to dismount and sends you on your way. Turn to **296**.

269

You tiptoe forward stealthily and pick up three of the scales which the dragon has shed. Each is as long as a man's forearm. Cautiously, you tiptoe out of the cave and continue up the mountain. Turn to 310.

270

The trail winds between the spurs of two hills and plunges down into a moist and mossy dell. At the bottom, a large dew pond, covered with algae, is shaded by the boughs of a horse-chestnut tree. Your attention is caught by a weak cry. An old woman is up to her neck in the middle of the pool. Her matted hair is streaked green with the scum of the pool. 'I'm drowning! Help me, I'm tangled in the weeds!' she begs piteously. If you help her, turn to 230. If you decide to ignore her and hurry on, turn to 65.

271

You catch it by surprise and strike it a mighty blow. It hisses in rage and pain and lunges at you with its rapier. You must fight the ENVOY OF DEATH. Each time it strikes you, you lose 1 SKILL point as well as the normal STAMINA loss.

ENVOY OF DEATH   SKILL 8   STAMINA 4

If you win, turn to 254.

272

'Well, how would we know, then?' says Scarface. The others laugh at you and turn their backs. If you want to go back to the barman and ask him the way to the Thieves' Guild, turn to **295**. If you would rather tap Scarface on the shoulder and say, 'Come on now, I won't tell anyone,' turn to **167**.

273

You come to the door of the Sage's house and knock. After a few moments a manservant opens the door. You explain that you have come to see the Sage. The manservant asks you for the token. Do you have the token? If you do, turn to **6**. If not, turn to **131**.

274

You thread your way through the moss-covered tombs and headstones. As you approach the light, it shimmers and moves towards you, floating in the darkness. You are entranced. The will-o'-the-wisp draws you, mesmerized, towards a large grey tomb. A withered hand thrusts through the earth beneath your feet and grabs your ankle. You hack at it but yet another mouldering arm grips you. There is a grating noise as a fiendish GHOUL staggers from the tomb before you. Other zombies erupt from their earthy graves around you. In your panic, you find the strength to rip yourself out of the ghastly grasp of the zombies – but the ghoul is almost upon you! You must fight it.

GHOUL   SKILL 7   STAMINA 8

If you defeat the Ghoul within five combat rounds, turn to **343**. If it is still alive after five rounds turn to **298**.

275

'You dare to threaten the Lord of the Skies, puny man-thing?' he bellows. Before you can reply he utters a word in a strange language. A powerful gust of wind suddenly blows up and hits you. *Test your Luck*. If you are Lucky, turn to **93**. If you are Unlucky, turn to **112**.

276

There is a hushed silence, broken by Vagrant. 'That is indeed beyond price.' He suddenly barks out an order: 'We'll mount an expedition before they move the Talisman. It is market-day – a good time. Scarface, Jemmy the Rat, Bloodheart and young Lord Min, you will accompany our friend here.' Some hours later, when they have finished their preparations, you set off. As you leave, you see a piece of graffiti scrawled in blood on a wall: *There is no honour among thieves!* You resolve to be on your guard. Turn to **241**.

277

A small boulder catches you and knocks you off the narrow steps. Lose 2 STAMINA points. If you are still alive and have a Roc's feather, turn to **231**. If you haven't got a feather, turn to **263**.

278

You enter the jeweller's. It seems to be curiously lacking in things of real value. The jeweller, a small man with a monocle, is just locking the large safe behind his counter. As he reaches for the closed sign, before you have the chance to speak, the three thieves you overheard burst into the shop, brandishing swords. Will you seek to get in with the thieves by capturing the jeweller (turn to **309**), or leap to the jeweller's aid and attack the thieves (turn to **286**)?

You slip inside the huge building and walk cautiously down empty corridors. You find a reading-room and decide to look at some of the scrolls. You find one which tells you that the women who brought you to Greyguilds worship Fell-Kyrinla. Another lists the different types of magic and the names given to those who practise them: warlocks, shamans, witches, necromancers, elementalists, thaumaturgists, demonists, cabalists, spellbinders and many more. The necromancers' magic interests you, for these are the death-magicians who perform human sacrifices and other unspeakable abominations in their pursuit of power. Then you notice a red book bound in strange multi-coloured scales. It seems to beckon you. Will you open the tome (turn to **262**), or leave before you are discovered (turn to **186**)?

280

You introduce yourself to the motley group of villains. They do not reply. You persevere, saying that you only wish to speak to them for a few moments. One of them, whose face is marked by a jagged scar, running from ear to chin, fixes you with a stare and grates, 'We don't care for the law, so watch yourself. You could be dead before you knew we'd moved.' Will you:

Ask them the way to the Thieves' Guild?	Turn to 145
Say you need help with some unfinished business?	Turn to 246
Boldly retort that their threats don't scare you?	Turn to 167

281

Scarface laughs. They remove their hands from their daggers and a young man appears from behind you and sits down. 'Of course we are thieves,' he says. 'What is the Red Dragon if not a den of thieves?' They invite you to join them for a drink, which you do. One of them tells you that the entrance to the Thieves' Guild is through an open storm-drain which leads into the sewers near Trader's Row. You ask if it is possible to go there right away, but they say no and you agree to meet them there at midday tomorrow. You begin to chat. Turn to 169.

282

You struggle up the nearest hill and halt at its summit. You have a few moments to catch your breath, before the first Orcs are upon you. Luckily, being no more than an undisciplined mob, they run at you one at a time. You must fight the first three in order. The third is apparently their leader, a huge broad brute with curving yellow tusks and a jagged-edged scimitar.

	SKILL	STAMINA
First ORC	5	6
Second ORC	5	4
Leader ORC	7	7

If you win, turn to 111.

283

You are padding silently along the landing towards the stairs which lead down, when a loud pealing of bells fills the air. 'The alarm,' snarls Scarface. You freeze. Looking back you are astonished to find that you cannot see the thieves, who you thought were behind you. All you can see are shadows. You are on your own. Will you go back to find the thieves (turn to 213), or run down the stairs ahead of you (turn to 180)?

284

Nothing happens. Turn to 292.

285

The Dragon bellows with pain but the thick scales on its back give it some protection even from Dragonsbane. Its tail whips round and catches you across the shoulder. Lose 2 STAMINA points. A wave of fear hits you as the Dragon turns its head, its yellow slitted eyes glinting with malice and pain. 'For that cowardly blow you shall die,' it roars. Will you:

Run back down the tunnel	Turn to 335
Try to grab some scales?	Turn to 398
Try to grab some of the dragon's treasure?	Turn to 38

286

Two of the thieves, thick-set bruisers in brown leather breeches, turn to face you, while the third, a thin weasel-faced man, goes for the jeweller. You must fight the two thieves together.

	SKILL	STAMINA
First THIEF	6	7
Second THIEF	5	6

If you kill one of the thieves, turn to 299.

287

The going is difficult and the darkening skies do nothing to raise your spirits. The Talisman becomes heavier with every step and the pouring rain soaks you to the skin. You are almost thankful when night comes and you can burrow down in the dead bracken. Unfortunately, your sleep is broken by a wild neighing. You jump up to see a massive black stallion, its eyes pits of fire, galloping towards you. It snorts clouds of glowing cinders as it strains at the bit. Its rider, a dark spectral figure, is hunched and twisted and seems to have no substance. You can sense the hatred it feels for all living things. Will you run from it, hoping it cannot charge across the broken ground (turn to **219**), or light a torch and stand your ground (turn to **207**)?

288

The man is a monk of the Order of the Scarlet Mantis, an expert in unarmed combat. He kicks and punches with deadly force. Each time he wins an attack round roll one die – if you throw a 5 or a 6 turn to **366**.

MONK OF THE
SCARLET MANTIS   SKILL 9   STAMINA 8

If you win, turn to **325**.

289

You step out, squinting against the bright light of the late afternoon sun. Add 1 LUCK point for visiting the Red Dragon Inn and living to tell the tale. You are back in the Street of Seven Sins. If you have met a Sage and he has invited you to dinner, you may turn to **229**. If you have not been invited, or do not wish to go, you may go down a side street called Cobbler's Walk, heading west (turn to **195**), or go down Merchant Street, heading north-west (turn to **394**).

290

In the flickering torchlight you read an inscription on the rectangular pillar.

Put yourself in the place of the monkey.
To the left is danger; the idle shall act.

Suddenly the three pillars disappear. You step back in amazement. The room remains empty and nothing else untoward happens, so you decide to leave. Turn to **339**.

291

'Where is this priceless jewellery stashed?' demands Vagrant. If you tell them to follow you and you'll show them, turn to **349**. If you tell them that it lies in the temple to Fell-Kyrinla, turn to **333**.

292

A spray of brightly coloured light speeds from Thaum's hands into your eyes, dazzling you. Cassandra stabs you neatly in the heart as Tyutchev cleaves your head from your shoulders. Turn to **109**.

293

You wait for some time, trying to ignore the growing ache in your muscles. Nothing happens. You decide to risk breaking cover and cross the river. Turn to **331**.

294

At this they leap up, whipping out their blades, and move to attack. Turn to **368**.

295

The barman says, 'I will tell you, but it will cost you six gold pieces and not a silver less.' If you have the money and wish to pay him, turn to **323**. If you do not have the money or do not wish to pay him, turn to **312**.

296

You walk into the city along a street called Moorgate. Many of the buildings are quite grand, built of light grey stone. The streets are crowded with a mixture of people shopping and young men and women carrying books and scrolls. Will you walk down a continuation of Moorgate, called Store Street (turn to **357**), or turn left into Smith Street (turn to **303**)?

297

The only people in sight hurry away, not looking at you. The footsteps come on and a dull, rasping voice intones, 'I am a spirit of the dead. We are beyond number.' Suddenly, a terrible blow knocks you backwards. Lose 2 STAMINA points. You must fight the UNSEEN STALKER.

UNSEEN STALKER   SKILL 9   STAMINA 8

If you win, turn to **250**.

298

You are still struggling with the Ghoul when you see the other Zombies closing in on you. Soon you are surrounded. A score of cold, dead hands grasp you and you are laid struggling in a newly dug grave. You scream as the earth is piled upon you. You are entering the wastelands of Death.

With a shout of victory, the jeweller steps back from the fallen body of his assailant, a bloodied short-sword in his hand. You are surprised that such a small old man is so skilful. Seeing this, your other opponent throws down his sword and runs out of the shop. You may pick up the thief's sword. The jeweller turns to you, his monocle swinging at his waist, and thanks you. He reaches behind the counter and hands you a leather pouch containing 10 gold pieces and a small velvet-covered box. Inside the box is a magnificent ruby. 'No one can call Oliol the Jeweller a miser,' he says. Scarcely believing your good fortune, you thank him and leave. Gain 1 LUCK point. Turn to 304.

300

As you walk on down the road, leaving all human habitation behind, it begins to rain heavily, transforming the dirt road into a morass of mud. By afternoon you decide to leave the road and head east, through the wilderness. After a hard day's trek, you camp for the night. Your sleep is fitful. You dream of Hawkana, clad in a funeral robe, her wounds still bleeding. She is standing at the edge of the Valley of Death, her hair streaming in a howling wind. She beckons you to follow, then turns and walks down into the blasted desolation of the valley. You wake up feeling on edge and drained of energy. Lose 2 STAMINA points and turn to 116.

301

As soon as you wound Tyutchev, you notice Thaum gesturing. Tyutchev becomes invisible. As you start back in surprise, Cassandra is upon you, her sword darting at you. Tyutchev reappears behind you, raising his sword to strike and Thaum is gesturing again. You feel threatened from all sides and you are hard pressed to defend yourself. Do you wish to call upon a God for aid (turn to 330), or do you think you can triumph by the skill of your own hand (turn to 292)?

302

You step forward and in the flickering torchlight read an inscription on the square pillar:

Furthest from the poison of the scarab beetle,
You will find a venom more deadly than dragon fire.

As you ponder the meaning of this strange message, a trickle of dust falls into your hair. As you look up, the ceiling begins to descend with a roar. Oiled spikes slide down towards you, protruding from the rock. A crushed skeleton is impaled on one of them. You jump forward as, with a grating rumble, a slab of rock starts to fall across the exit ahead. Your only hope is to throw yourself through the narrowing gap. Roll two dice. If the total is equal to or less than your SKILL score turn to **103**. If the total is greater than your SKILL score turn to **215**.

303

You stride down Smith Street. Next door to a tinker's shop you see what appears to be an armourers. Do you wish to go in (turn to **139**), or pass by (turn to **104**)?

304

You continue down Silver Street, past the jeweller's, which is closed, and turn left into a tree-lined avenue called Booker's Walk. Two very grand buildings, built of blocks of grey stone, stand on either side of the road. A group of young people in blue togas, escorted by a white-haired old man in pale blue robes, enters the building opposite. A flag showing books and scrolls is flying from the nearest building. It appears to be a library. Will you see what information the library has to offer (turn to 346), or investigate the other building to find out what the young people are doing (turn to 279)?

305

As you walk across the sawdust-covered tiles towards the door, you hear Tyutchev say to the barman, 'Who was that frightened rabbit?' He walks over to the thieves. Do you want to hurry out of this den of thieves, thankful to be alive (turn to 289), or draw your sword and shout 'Who's frightened?' (turn to 294)?

306

The alchemist gives you the jar of ointment in exchange for the gold. 'Rub it into your arms and chest right away. It will make your skin as tough as bark for a week.' You take his advice. As soon as you have rubbed on all the ointment, your skin begins to burn. The pain is excruciating and your skin blisters. Lose 2 STAMINA points. If you are still alive, Alembic says, mildly concerned, 'Alas, something must have curdled. It will pass. I am a fair man. Here are your seven gold pieces. Perhaps you would like to try something else?' You accept your money back. If you have not tried them already, you can buy any of his other wares:

Fortunate Luckstone – 10 gold
  pieces.   Turn to **266**
Vapours of Speed – 10 gold pieces.   Turn to **233**
Elixir of Life – 12 gold pieces.   Turn to **360**
Or would you rather leave his
  shop in disgust?   Turn to **28**

307

You hide yourself in the bushes, hoping that the Elves will be unable to follow your trail. *Test your Luck*. If you are Lucky, turn to **293**. If you are Unlucky, turn to **344**.

308

You flatten yourself against the cliff just in time. The boulders hurtle past and explode as they hit the step just below you. You carry on, warily climbing up the steps. Turn to **192**.

309

The jeweller reaches for a sword behind the counter but you are too quick for him. You grab the sword and hold its edge to his throat. He tenses up and says, 'There's my safe. Take it all but don't hurt me!' He points to the safe at the back of the room. One of the thieves, a thin weasel of a man, binds the jeweller. You may keep the jeweller's sword, if you wish. The other two, mean-looking thugs in brown breeches, look you over coolly. Will you demand your pick of the loot (turn to **66**), or ask for a small share of the booty (turn to **354**)?

310

Do you have a gourd filled with Gum of an Amber Pine? If you do, turn to **385**. If you do not, turn to **369**.

311

The man is a monk of the Order of the Scarlet
Mantis, an expert in unarmed combat. He attacks
you without hesitation. He kicks and punches with
deadly force. Each time he wins an Attack Round,
roll one die – if you throw a 5 or a 6 turn to **366**.

MONK OF THE
SCARLET MANTIS   SKILL 9   STAMINA 8

If you win, go to **325**.

312

Unfortunately the thieves have overheard you. The
youngest moves soundlessly behind you, hidden
by one of the tapestries. A searing pain rips into
your back. He has stabbed you with a poisoned
dagger. You sink to the floor, unable to move. The
young thief callously pockets your purse. Turn to
109.

313

As you walk across the barren heath, the sky turns grey and specks of rain interrupt your thoughts. You press on as the rain becomes heavier, head bowed to keep your face dry. You fail to notice a winged monster swooping down towards you. You are knocked to the ground – lose 2 STAMINA points. If you are still alive, you pick yourself up and find yourself face to face with a winged lion with the head of an eagle. It is bent on making a meal of you. You must fight the GRIFFIN.

GRIFFIN   SKILL 8   STAMINA 14

If you reduce its STAMINA to 6 or less, turn to **94**.

314

You make a grab for some of the scales, but trip, in your haste, over a golden chest filled with black pearls. The Dragon turns and as you are struggling to your feet it breathes on you. Rolling jets of flame consume you and char you to a cinder. Turn to **43**.

315

'Oh yes?' says Vagrant. 'What is this thing?' If you say you're not prepared to tell what it is, but it lies in the temple of Fell-Kyrinla, turn to **370**. If you tell them it's the Talisman of Death and you are prepared to share the spoils when you get it, turn to **276**.

316

'You don't walk out on Tyutchev!' They leap up, whipping out their blades, and move to attack. Turn to 368.

317

The mellow voice of the Dragon is pleasant and you find yourself speaking freely to it. The Dragon explains that it is the guardian of the portal and you tell it of your need to pass through. Its beguiling charm carries you away and when it tells you to leave your weapons before setting off to the portal you do as it suggests. As you turn your back, the Dragon pounces and snaps your neck like a twig. Turn to 43.

318

Still seated behind Elvira, you are riding into the City of Learning, Greyguilds, along a street called Moorgate. Many of the buildings are quite grand, built of a light grey stone. You see a mixture of people. There are men wearing light blue togas who are Sages and professors from the Guilds of Learning. Other groups of young men and women are carrying books and scrolls. There are eight of the warrior-women still with you. Will you jump down and try to fight your way free (turn to 362), or change your mind and go quietly to meet Hawkana (turn to 351)?

319

You struggle to tear yourself away from the pool, but a gentle and soothing voice suggests that you fall into a peaceful sleep. You feel nothing as you enter the cool green water. You are charmed by the WILLOW WEIRD. It thrashes you with its branches as you sink beneath the water. Lose 4 STAMINA points. The pain shocks you out of your reverie and you struggle out of the pool. Looking up, you can see two large green eyes staring at you from the trunk of the willow. You must fight it.

WILLOW WEIRD   SKILL 8   STAMINA 12

If you make four successful attacks, turn to **26**.

320

The other two thieves run for it when they see how skilfully you dispatched their ferocious friend. You are left alone in the shop with the dead jeweller. His eyes seem to gaze at you in mute reproach. Will you put up the closed sign and try to open the jeweller's safe (turn to **341**), or leave immediately in case you are accused of murder (turn to **304**)?

321

In the flickering torchlight you can see an inscription on the circular pillar.

> *Behind the symbol on the first door*
> *Lies that which you risk your life for.*

Suddenly the three pillars disappear. You step back in amazement, but nothing else untoward happens and the room remains empty, so you decide to leave. Turn to **339**.

322

'Where did the caravan come from – the Spires of Foreshadowing, perhaps?' demands the Captain of the patrol. Where will you say it came from?

The Spires	Turn to **173**
The City of the Runes of Doom	Turn to **123**
Serakub	Turn to **191**

323

He takes the money greedily and says, 'The entrance lies through an open storm-drain which leads into the sewers near Trader's Row. I wouldn't go there now, if I were you, but it will be safe around midday tomorrow.' You thank him and prepare to leave. Just then, two new customers enter the gloomy ale cellar. The first is a very tall, wiry, man whose frame is wreathed in a black cloak which seems to deepen the darkness around him. The only hint of colour is his hair, very curly and dyed bright corn-yellow. The second is a handsome young woman dressed in a bizarre patchwork of armour. The barman mutters under his breath and then forces his face into a smile. 'Tyutchev, Cassandra, welcome!' he shouts obsequiously. He moves to the other end of the bar to serve Tyutchev, who orders a carafe of Spirits of Ra. Cassandra sits at a nearby empty table and Tyutchev joins her. Will you:

Turn away from the bar and leave?	Turn to 363
Sit down and finish your ale?	Turn to 2
Introduce yourself to Tyutchev and Cassandra?	Turn to 374

324

You make a grab for one of the scales but trip over a golden goblet studded with fire-opals. Recovering your balance, you snatch up three of the scales before the Dragon can turn round and run back down the narrow twisting tunnel. You leave the cave as fast as you can and continue up the mountain. Turn to 310.

325

Your blade slashes him across the chest and he slumps to the ground. You step over his body and walk past the cart. Looking back, to your surprise you see the monk has risen to his feet and is running away! Obviously he was feigning death. You shrug your shoulders and go on. Turn to 392.

326

You are nearing mountains which stretch away in a haze of purple to the south. Ahead of you lies the plateau. Suddenly, a dark shadow falls around you. Looking up you see an enormous bird swooping down towards you. Its beak alone is larger than you. Will you:

Stand to fight it?	Turn to **18**
Kneel to fight it?	Turn to **27**
Lie prone?	Turn to **37**

327

They betray a flicker of interest. Tyutchev calmly says, 'I have no time for such adventures,' but his curiosity is obvious. You begin to think you may have made a mistake in telling them and get up to leave. As you climb the steps to the street you see Tyutchev walking over to the thieves. Turn to **289**.

328

As you climb the steps the temperature and humidity increase. Dripping with sweat, you look up and see that the lip of the cliff is only sixty metres above you. Suddenly, several boulders crash down from the top. Roll two dice. If the total is less than or equal to your SKILL score, turn to **308**. If the total is greater than your SKILL score, turn to **277**.

329

You search the two thieves and find 6 gold pieces. Turn to **304**.

330

Which god will you call on?

Avatar the One	Turn to 347
Lifespirit	Turn to 284
Rocheval, God of the Paladins	Turn to 361
The All-Mother	Turn to 248
Fate	Turn to 389

331

The river flows out of the hills into a wide plain, where it turns north. You strike out west across the wild grasslands. Just when you think you have finally lost your pursuers, you notice a group of figures closing fast. Cursing under your breath, you realize that they are on to you again. Doggedly, you force yourself on, but the strain takes its toll. Lose 2 STAMINA points. Just as you are stealing yourself to turn and face your fell adversaries, you see a cloud of dust ahead. You can soon make out a group of twenty horsemen. They wheel their steeds towards you and the drumming of hoofs carries to you over the breeze as they canter in your direction. Seeing this, the Elves seem to give up the chase and fall back, obviously unwilling to encounter the riders. You are thankful to see the back of them and decide to wait for the riders to approach. As they get nearer, you can see that this is a band of warrior-women, clad in chainmail and studded leather armour. Their faces look grim and unwelcoming as they wheel around you, forming a close circle. Their Captain spurs her horse forward and tersely demands what you are doing out here, along the edge of the moor. What will you do:

Ask them to aid you in your quest?	Turn to **101**
Say you are from another world?	Turn to **73**
Say you are the sole survivor of an ambushed caravan?	Turn to **322**
Pretend that you are deaf and dumb?	Turn to **35**
Demand they escort you to Greyguilds-on-the-Moor?	Turn to **95**

332

The wall opens to reveal a blank wall of rock. It is a false door. You close it and the monkey's grin seems to mock you. You may choose another door. Which will you choose?

The serpent door	Turn to **168**
The scarab beetle door	Turn to **377**
The dragon door	Turn to **352**

333

Vagrant replies, 'Are you mad? Nothing is worth raiding the temple of Fell-Kyrinla for.' If you tell them about the Talisman of Death, turn to **276**. If you decide to call their bluff, saying that you will find someone else to share the spoils with, turn to **367**.

334

You ride into the City of Learning, Greyguilds, along a street called Moorgate. Many of the buildings are quite grand, built of light grey stone. You see a mixture of people in the streets. There are some men wearing light blue togas who are Sages and professors from the Guilds of Learning. Other groups of young men and women are carrying books and scrolls. You realize that, unarmed as you are, you are no match for these women and have no alternative but to go with them. Turn to **351**.

335

The Dragon makes no attempt to follow you and you run out of the cave and climb towards the summit. Turn to **369**.

336

The sage directs you to *The Book of the Gods*, a large leather-bound tome, inlaid with gold leaf. Turning the gilt-edged pages you realize the Gods of Orb are many. You recognize a symbol on one of the pages as being the token borne by the warrior-women. Their goddess is Fell-Kyrinla, swordsmistress of the heavens. She is sworn to oppose Rocheval the Good, God of Paladins. To your excitement you discover a reference to the Talisman: *Some believe that it can be used to command the undead minions of Death.* Turning the page you come to a reference to the All-Mother, *Nature herself, preserver of life, who cares for all.* Then you see a bizarrely illustrated page dealing with *Anarchil, breaker of edifices, who spurns order.* You are just learning of *Avatar the One, essence of light,* when you realize that it has grown dark while you were reading. You thank the Sage and leave quickly, hoping to find a safe place to sleep. Turn to **186**.

337

They seem to lose interest in you and leave your table to talk to the six thieves. You decide to leave the Red Dragon, while you still can. Turn to **289**.

338

He does not let you pass. Will you step aside and invite him to pass first (turn to **379**), or ask him less politely to move out of the way (turn to **311**)?

339

You try all the doors, but you can only get one of them to open. You seem to have no choice and you go through into the room beyond. It is a wide hall, stretching away to the left and right. In the centre of the room stands a hideous idol. Its base is the coiled tail of a huge serpent. Its muscular torso sprouts four clawed arms, two gruesome heads and bat-like wings. An inscription on the floor reads, *Damolh, son of the God Nil, Mouth of the Void*. In the opposite wall are four doors, two to the left and two to the right. Each door bears a symbol. Furthest from you on the left is a green serpent. The next door bears a grinning monkey; the third, a black scarab beetle and the fourth, furthest to your right, a red dragon, breathing fire. Which door will you open:

The serpent door?	Turn to **168**
The monkey door?	Turn to **332**
The scarab beetle door?	Turn to **377**
The dragon door?	Turn to **352**

340

'I am a thief, among other things,' says Tyutchev. 'Why do you wish to meet thieves?' You tell him that you have some unfinished business and need some help. 'Ah yes,' he says, 'but I am needed at my temple. I am not interested.' Will you take your leave and go up the steps out into the street (turn to **289**), or mention that the business involves the Talisman of Death (turn to **327**)?

341

As you reach for the safe, a blinding sheet of flame envelops you. The safe was fire-trapped and you have been fried. Turn to **109**.

342

Tyutchev steps between you. His sword is almost as tall as you and he hefts it negligently in one hand. Cassandra steps back, clasping her arm. 'You've a difficult fight on your hands, Tyutchev,' she gasps.

TYUTCHEV   SKILL 10   STAMINA 12

If you reduce Tyutchev's STAMINA to 4 or less turn to **355**.

343

With a mighty slash, your sword bites into the pale, slimy neck of the Ghoul, decapitating it. It slumps to the floor, truly dead at last. As fast as you can, you spring past the questing arms of the lumbering zombies and dash back to the wall, knowing you must find the postern gate as soon as possible. Turn to **99**.

344

Within moments you can hear the Elves swarming round you. They begin driving their swords into the bushes. Realizing you have little choice but to face them, you stand up and rush at them with your sword drawn. One of them makes a strange gesture. A sudden pain grips you and you fall to the ground. The Elves are using foul sorcery. Unable to resist, you watch helplessly as they bind you hand and foot. You are to be taken back to the depths of the Rift, never to see daylight again. Your quest ends here.

345

In the flickering torchlight you can see an inscription on the square pillar:

Furthest from the poison of the scarab beetle
You will find a venom more deadly than dragon fire.

Suddenly the three pillars disappear. You step back in amazement. The room remains empty and nothing else untoward happens, so you decide to leave. Turn to **339**.

346

The entrance hall of the library is filled with desks at which scribes are working, copying books and scrolls. Reclining on a plush window-seat is a wrinkled old fellow in the pale blue robes of a scholar. You feel out of place, wearing armour in the quiet of the library, where the stillness is broken only by the scratching of pens. 'Welcome to the largest library in the Manmarch,' says the Sage. 'Choose any tome or scroll you may wish to peruse. Perhaps I may be of assistance. What is your field of study?' Will you ask to read something about the Gods (turn to **336**), or ask to read about the history of Greyguilds (turn to **196**)?

347

Nothing happens. Turn to **292**.

348

The dirt you have thrown splatters across an invisible form. It outlines the shape of a thin man-like being about three metres tall. It moves towards you, almost mechanically, until it towers above you and you realize it is about to attack. You must fight the UNSEEN STALKER.

UNSEEN STALKER   SKILL 7   STAMINA 8

If you win turn to **250**.

349

Vagrant sneers, 'Who do you think you are – a God? Vagar the Deceiver himself? Get thee gone.' He waves his arm dismissively. Turn to **367**.

350

You notice that the base of the sarcophagus is hollow and you break through it to find a tunnel below. You jump down and feel your way along its damp-walled windings. At last, you see a circle of daylight ahead. You emerge on to the steps again, some way above the roaring waterfall, and begin to climb. Turn to **328**.

351

You are taken along Moorgate, past various food and pottery shops, and then down bustling Store Street. They turn right down Guard Street and come to a halt outside a squat grey building. It is the watch-house. The patrol dismounts and you are ushered inside. Turn to **78**.

352

You open the door and step through into a passage. You have only gone a few steps when you hear the rattle of a falling chain as a portcullis drops behind you, blocking the tunnel. You can only go on into a small room ahead of you. It is a dank crypt, at the end of which lies a sarcophagus, thickly covered in grey mould. You search every nook and cranny, but you cannot find a way out. You are trapped. Eventually you decide to lift the lid of the sarcophagus. The rank and fetid air, trapped inside since time immemorial, smells sickly sweet. Inside lie the mummified remains of a warrior, his skin stretched taught over brittle bones. His skeletal hand is curled around an ancient scimitar encrusted with emeralds and an ebony spear with an ivory tip lies across his chest. Will you take the sword (turn to 387) or the spear (turn to 395)?

353

Your last blow has drawn a gout of blood from Tyutchev's side. He jumps back and says, 'Anarchil, breaker of edifices, aid me.' He is calling upon his God. Before you can strike the killing blow the cellar starts to shake. An earthquake opens great cracks in the floor. There is a roar of tumbling masonry and the inn is filled with dust. In the confusion, Tyutchev and Cassandra make good their escape. When the quake has stopped you climb the steps and leave. Turn to 289.

354

The weasel-faced thief buries his sword in the unfortunate jeweller's back and says to you, as if nothing had happened, 'Well, I don't know – you're not even a member of the Guild. I'll tell you what, though, if you open the safe we'll give you a share. It is protected by a magical Glyph of Warding. You must say, "I am undone", to cancel the power that guards the safe.' If you go to the safe and do as he says – hoping to get first pick of anything inside – turn to 341. If you refuse and invite him to try it, turn to 364.

355

Your last blow has drawn a gout of blood from Tyutchev's side. He jumps back and cries, 'Anarchil, breaker of edifices, aid me.' Before you can strike the killing blow the cellar starts to shake. An earthquake opens great cracks in the floor. There is a roar of tumbling masonry and the inn is filled with dust. In the confusion Tyutchev and Cassandra make good their escape. When the quake has stopped you climb the steps, throwing the cursed tiger charm to the ground, and head out into the blinding sunlight. Turn to 289.

356

The Dragon says it is guardian of the portal and that it will allow you to pass through with the Talisman. In its rich mellifluous voice it says, 'You will have no further use for your weapons, leave them here.' Will you:

Do as it bids and lay down your weapons?	Turn to **373**
Run forward to attack?	Turn to **146**
Run for your life?	Turn to **380**

357

You are now in Store Street. It is crowded with shoppers but your attention is drawn to a woman in green robes, who is looking at you speculatively. Her straight hair is cut fairly short and she is wearing no ornaments. She crosses the street, and asks politely, in a quiet but clear voice, 'I believe you are a stranger in this city. Who are you and where have you come from?' Will you tell her that you are on a holy quest and have crossed the wilderness (turn to **198**), or say that you are just passing through and start to walk briskly on (turn to **130**)?

358

Its mellow voice carries across the wind: 'I know nothing of Death; he cannot touch me. I am the guardian placed here by the Gods, nothing more, nothing less.' Will you tell it about the Talisman and its importance (turn to **211**), or run to attack the Dragon (turn to **382**)?

359

You run as fast as you can but your exertions have left you exhausted. Unable to find a hiding-place, you have to turn to face the Dark Elves who are almost upon you. One of them gestures strangely. A sudden pain grips you and you fall to the ground. The Elves are using foul sorcery. Unable to resist, you can do nothing as they bind you hand and foot. You are to be taken back to the depths of the Rift, never to see daylight again. Your quest ends here.

360

The alchemist gives you the bottle in exchange for the gold, telling you to drink it while it is fresh. You decide to do so there and then. It has the pungent odour of wild garlic. Drinking it, you feel invigorated. Increase your *Initial* STAMINA score by 2 points. You can now restore your STAMINA to this new maximum. You feel your money has been well spent as you have been given a new lease of life. If you have any money left, you may purchase any other items which you haven't tried:

Barkskin – 7 gold pieces.	Turn to 306
Fortunate Luckstone – 10 gold pieces.	Turn to 266
Vapours of Speed – 10 gold pieces.	Turn to 233
Or are you ready to leave and continue on your way?	Turn to 28

361

Nothing happens. Turn to **292**.

362

You jump down and back into a corner between two shops, so that they cannot all attack you at once. The Captain and Elvira dismount and draw their swords while another turns and gallops back to Moorgate. You must fight these two first.

	SKILL	STAMINA
CAPTAIN	8	10
ELVIRA	6	8

In any round, if the Captain's Attack Strength is 10 or more and she wounds you, turn to **393**. If you win, turn to **376**.

363

'Stay!' says Tyutchev, arrogantly gesturing you back to your seat. Will you keep going (turn to **316**), or do as he bids and return to your stool (turn to **374**)?

364

'Shame,' he says, 'you would have been killed.' At this the two large thieves attack you. You must fight them.

	SKILL	STAMINA
First THIEF	6	7
Second THIEF	5	6

If you kill one of the thieves, turn to **391**.

365

Their village is composed of several elegant buildings made from wattle, daubed with clay. A deep dry moat and spiked palisade surround it. You are led through the village to what must be the Headhog's dwelling, a two-storeyed building, part of which is built from crumbling green stone. A huge mud wallow lies nearby. The Headhog sits on a carved stone throne, his muscles rippling under his blue-black skin. He wears a red robe fastened at his thick neck with a necklace of amber. He seems at ease but he demands to know why you, a human, are on the plateau. If you say that you mean no harm – you are searching for the portals on Mount Starreach – turn to **110**. If you tell him you are looking for a lost city, turn to **90**.

366

With a grunt of effort, the monk kicks your wrist, disarming you with his left foot, and scissors his right foot into your chin before his other foot has touched the ground. You go out like a light. You regain consciousness when water is splashed on to your face by the driver of the ox-cart. Your head is still ringing. 'I'm afraid he robbed you,' says the peasant. Frantically, you check for the Talisman, but the monk has only taken the ring you found on Hawkana. Turn to **392**.

367

'Good luck to you, then,' says Scarface. The thieves are still pointing their crossbows at you. Vagrant leaves and you decide it would be prudent to do the same. There seems to be nothing else you can do except tackle the temple to Fell-Kyrinla alone. You set off in search of it. Turn to **383**.

368

Tyutchev's sword is almost as tall as you are and he wields it negligently in one hand. Cassandra's glows coldly. Each time she hits you must subtract 3 STAMINA points.

	SKILL	STAMINA
TYUTCHEV	10	12
CASSANDRA	9	10

If you reduce Cassandra's STAMINA to 4 or less she drops back and Tyutchev moves in to cover her. If you reduce Tyutchev's STAMINA to 4 or less turn to **353**.

You climb on, gasping for breath in the thin air. At last you reach the flat summit. The panorama is incredible. The whole plateau lies below you like a table, a collage of tropical forests, mountains and huge lakes, which glisten in the sun. Thirty metres away is a rectangle of shimmering silver, hanging in the air, unsupported. You realize that this is the portal. As you step towards it you hear the rushing of wind. Looking up you see the ancient Red Dragon. It lands beside the portal. Outside its lair the Dragon is even more impressive and fearsome. Warmth and power seem to radiate from its body. 'I am bound by the Gods to guard the portal. I will live until the day that somebody passes through. It is a shame, but I cannot allow you to pass,' he says with relish. You step forward to do battle, as he draws a deep breath. With a bellow he empties his cavernous lungs. Rolling jets of flame engulf you, before you can attack him. You are charred to a cinder. Your quest ends in sight of your goal. Turn to **43**.

370

'Thank you,' says Vagrant. 'Now that we know where to go we have no further need of you.' He snaps his fingers. A volley of crossbow bolts find their mark and you crash to the ground, dead. Turn to **109**.

371

The mummy collapses into a pile of splintered bones and ragged linen. You examine the scimitar and the spear. The spear has the word 'Dragons-bane' carved on its shaft and is obviously magical. You decide to take it and you may add 1 to your SKILL score when wielding it in battle. Turn to **350**.

372

Alembic greets you and says cheerfully, 'You look like an adventurous person. Would you like to buy something?' You inquire what he has to offer. He shows you the following things, each marked with a price. Do you want to buy:

A small potion-bottle marked
'Elixir of Life' for 12 gold pieces?   Turn to **360**

A jar of ointment labelled
'Barkskin' for 7 gold pieces?   Turn to **306**

A 'Fortunate Luckstone' for
10 gold pieces?   Turn to **266**

A small vial labelled 'Vapours of
Speed' for 10 gold pieces?   Turn to **233**

If you decide you would rather turn and leave, turn to **28**.

373

The Dragon allows you to leave but, as you go, you fancy that you see a glint of malice in its eye. Fear spurs you on. You hurry quickly out of the cave and continue the climb to the summit. Turn to **369**.

374

They tell you their names are Tyutchev and Cassandra. Tyutchev says, 'You are a newcomer – what brings you to the Red Dragon?' The beautiful Cassandra takes a dagger from her boot and starts to toss it end over end, catching it each time by the tip. As you consider your answer she tosses it again but does not catch it. It buries itself in the table, a centimetre from your hand. Will you:

Say that you wish to meet some thieves?	Turn to **340**
Say you came in for a drink?	Turn to **386**
Tell him to mind his own business?	Turn to **397**

375

Store Street is an extension of Moorgate, the road leading to the arch through which you entered the city. The market-day crowds are thronging the streets and you look around nervously. Will you:

Hasten down Store Street to the Moorgate arch?	Turn to **237**
Lie low in an alley until evening?	Turn to **126**
Or, if you had dinner with a Sage, ask the way to the cemetery?	Turn to **261**

376

The others ride away from you, raising a hue and cry as they go. You run along Store Street and then double back along a dark alley that parallels Moorgate, and conceal yourself behind some old barrels. After waiting for some time you dare to come out of hiding and walk carefully back on to Moorgate. Will you go down Store Street (turn to 357), or turn left into Smith Street (turn to 303)?

377

The door will not open. As you try again you hear a noise behind you. You wheel round in time to see the idol cracking open like an egg, scattering a thousand shards of rock across the room. Out writhes Damolh, the monstrous son of the God Nil, Mouth of the Void. He moves slowly but purposefully towards you. You fight him but he is invulnerable. Your sword makes no impression and you cannot do him harm. You realize your only chance is to escape through one of the doors. You jump back. Which door will you try:

The serpent door?	Turn to 168
The monkey door?	Turn to 390
The dragon door?	Turn to 352

378

The tunnel goes on, turning left and downwards. As you round the corner you come face to face with an immense Dragon. The heavy lids of its eyes are almost closed and small puffs of sulphurous smoke billow from its nostrils. It is about eighteen metres long and covered in red scales. Its long tail is curled around a vast hoard of treasure – gems, gold, goblets and vases lie higgledy-piggledy beneath its drowsy bulk. Will you:

Creep towards the Dragon?	Turn to **115**
Cast your spear at it, if you have one?	Turn to **82**
Go back to explore the side-tunnel?	Turn to **22**
Leave the cave and carry on up the mountain?	Turn to **369**
Try to steal some of the Dragon's treasure?	Turn to **38**

379

You step back and wave the monk through. He walks past arrogantly, without a word of thanks. Turn to **392**.

380

You run and a wave of fear hits you as the Dragon roars evilly, 'Until the portal then, manling.' You arrive safely at the cave mouth and continue the climb to the summit. Turn to **369**.

381

As you say the words and reach for the safe, a blinding sheet of flame envelops you. The safe was fire-trapped and you have been fried. Turn to **109**.

382

As you charge at the Dragon it breathes a tongue of rolling flame at you. You crouch behind your shield which protects you from the fiery blast. Before you can attack, the Dragon, roaring in anger, swipes at the shield with a massive claw. Roll two dice; if the total is less than your SKILL score, turn to **34**. If the total is equal to or greater than your SKILL score, turn to **79**.

383

You spot one of the warrior-women who you know are members of the temple of Fell-Kyrinla. Hoping she is on her way to the temple, you follow her at a distance. Eventually, you come to a building made of a white stone, with dark grey columns. Steps lead up to the entrance between two pillars and there is a guard at the top. What will you do:

Attack the guard?   Turn to **234**
Tell her you have a message for the
    High Priestess?   Turn to **202**

384

You hack your way through the undergrowth but dense thorn bushes make progress slow and difficult. You are soon panting for breath, and exertion has made you hungry. You must eat – cross one Provision off your Adventure Sheet. You do not gain any STAMINA from this meal. You battle on. Turn to 65.

385

Pausing in a gully, you examine the scales. You fit them together to form a shield and, using the gum of the amber pine, you bond them together. Turn to 69.

386

'Alone?' inquires Tyutchev. 'Strangers don't come to the Red Dragon just for a drink. Don't you know we're all thieves? What are you up to?' Will you tell him to mind his own business (turn to 397), or apologize, say you must have made a mistake and leave (turn to 289)?

387

As you try to draw the sword from the MUMMY's grasp, the fingers suddenly tighten into a grip of iron. The ancient corpse sits upright with a rustle of falling dust. You step back in horror as the Mummy rises from the sarcophagus clutching the scimitar and spear. It lumbers to attack you, for trying to rob its tomb. You must fight it.

MUMMY   SKILL 9   STAMINA 10

If you win, turn to **371**.

388

They ignore your threat and spur their horses through the fire at you. You cast the Talisman into the flames, but it remains untarnished. One of the Wraiths picks it from the glowing embers and touches you with it. Your soul is sucked into the Talisman and your body crumbles to dust. You are now just a part of the power of the Talisman.

389

You hear a voice speaking in your head, 'I will help you but, for now, Death will take you. What is destined to happen, must come to pass.' Turn to **292**.

390

The door opens to reveal a blank wall of rock. It is a false door. The monkey's grin seems to mock you. Before you can move, a heavy green coil loops itself around your chest. You are thrown on the floor and crushed by Damolh's powerful tail. His jackal heads start to feed off you while you are still alive and your spirit is sucked into the blackness of the void. Your quest ends here.

391

Seeing your deadly sword-play, the third thief bolts into the street. The other one pleads for mercy, throwing down his sword. 'I'll tell you what the right words are,' he gabbles. 'Just say, "I am a casket of iron and fire"!' Will you try the safe, using these words (turn to **381**), or order him to try the safe (turn to **399**)?

392

Dusk is deepening as you enter the cemetery. You begin to explore the city wall, looking for the postern gate. You do not look at the headstones for fear of finding your name at the head of an open grave. Your eye is caught by what looks like a lantern, hanging from a post in the midst of the graves. Will you walk over to the lantern (turn to 274), or ignore the lantern and continue searching along the wall (turn to 99)?

393

Wanting to take you alive, the Captain closes with you and slams her shield into your sword-arm. Before you can strike again she brings the hilt of her sword crashing into the side of your neck; you slump to the floor, stunned. Your arms are tied behind you and you are pushed on your way once more. Turn to 351.

394

You pass several markets where grain-merchants are dealing, but one small, drab shop looks more interesting – a board announces 'Alembic the Alchemist'. There is nothing in the window but a small plate with what look like five hazel nuts on it, and a stuffed lynx. Peering in, you see a man dressed in a white, sleeveless robe with a phoenix rising from flames embroidered on it. Will you enter the shop (turn to **372**), or go on your way (turn to **28**)?

395

You take the heavy spear and, looking closer, see that the word 'Dragonsbane' is carved on its shaft. It is obviously magical and you may add 1 to your SKILL score when wielding it. With a creak of old bones the MUMMY rises from the sarcophagus. It lumbers drunkenly towards you, clutching its scimitar, bent on destroying the despoiler of its tomb.

MUMMY   ·   SKILL 8   STAMINA 10

If you win turn to **350**.

396

You smash the skull into splinters of bone, but Mortphilio has not been idle. The walls of the parlour are not bamboo but are made from the bones of the necromancer's victims. He summons them forth to attack you. He is soon surrounded by skeletal warriors and you decide to run before you are overwhelmed. The only clear way is down a long stone corridor that leads to an archway across which a black blanket is draped. You run through, pushing the blanket aside and catch your breath in amazement. Turn to **97**.

397

'I think you're going to regret that,' says Tyutchev between gritted teeth. Cassandra says, softly, 'I think, stranger, it would be better if you begged his pardon, don't you?' What will you say: 'I'll not apologize to the likes of him' (turn to **294**), or 'Oh yes, I beg your pardon' (turn to **337**)?

398

Test your Luck. If you are Lucky turn to **324**. If you are Unlucky turn to **314**.

399

The thief says, sullenly, 'If I must,' and moves over to the safe. Suddenly he leaps acrobatically over the counter and is out of the shop like a flash. Will you try to open the safe saying, 'I am a casket of iron and fire' (turn to **381**), or leave the shop in case the thug tells the Watch you have killed the jeweller (turn to **304**)?

400

Before you step through the portal you drink in the splendid view of this fantastic and magical world for a little longer. The glittering lakes and emerald forests shimmer in a haze of heat. The Talisman is heavy at your chest. With a final prayer to the All-Mother you step into the silvery screen of the portal, remembering the four crusaders who gave you your quest. You meet no resistance as you pass through the screen. All goes dark and then a very different landscape lies before you. You are within a circle of standing stones. The smells, the air, the birdsong – everything seems strange but you know that you have found your way back to Earth. You are a hero, saviour of the world of Orb, but there is no one here to herald your return. As you step away from the standing stones, voices speak within your head. The two beings who summoned you to Orb are thanking you for saving the world. At last they tell you who they are. Time, Eldest Father, Youngest Son, and Fate, Keeper of the Balance, both Gods of Orb. As you leave this sacred place, their final words ring in your ears.

'We may call upon you again!'

More Fighting Fantasy in Puffins

1. THE WARLOCK OF FIRETOP MOUNTAIN

Steve Jackson and Ian Livingstone

Deep in the caverns beneath the threatening crags of Firetop Mountain, a powerful Warlock lives, guarding a mass of treasure – or so the rumour goes. Several adventurers like yourself have set off for Firetop Mountain, but none has returned. Do you dare to follow them? Who knows what terrors you may find!

2. THE CITADEL OF CHAOS

Steve Jackson

You are the star pupil of the Grand Wizard of Yore and your mission is to venture into the dark, doom-laden tower of the demi-sorcerer, Balthus Dire. Risking death at every turn of the passage, will you be able to overcome the six-headed Hydra, the peril of the Rhino-man and the deadly and mysterious Ganjees? With only your sword and your magical skills to aid you, your task is truly awesome.

3. THE FOREST OF DOOM

Ian Livingstone

Only the foolhardy would risk an encounter with the unknown perils that lurk in the murky depths of Darkwood Forest. Yet there is no alternative, for your quest is a desperate race against time to find the missing pieces of the legendary Hammer of Stonebridge – fashioned by Dwarfs to protect the villagers of Stonebridge against their ancient doom.

4. STARSHIP TRAVELLER

Steve Jackson

Sucked through the appalling nightmare of the Seltsian Void, the starship Traveller emerges at the other side of the black hole into an unknown universe. YOU are the captain of the Traveller and her fate lies in your hands. Will you be able to discover the way back to Earth from the alien peoples and planets you encounter, or will you and your crew be doomed to roam uncharted space forever?

5. CITY OF THIEVES

Ian Livingstone

Terror stalks the night as Zanbar Bone and his bloodthirsty Moon Dogs hold the prosperous town of Silverton to ransom. YOU are an adventurer, and the merchants of Silverton turn to you in their hour of need. Your mission takes you along dark, twisting streets where thieves, vagabonds and creatures of the night lie in wait to trap the unwary traveller.

6. DEATHTRAP DUNGEON

Ian Livingstone

Down in the twisting labyrinth of Fang, unknown horrors await you. Countless adventurers before you have taken up the challenge of the Trial of Champions, but not one has survived. Devised by the devilish mind of Baron Sukumvit, the labyrinth is riddled with fiendish traps and hideous creatures of darkness to trick and test your endurance.

7. ISLAND OF THE LIZARD KING

Ian Livingstone

Kidnapped by a vicious race of Lizard Men from Fire Island, the young men of Oyster Bay face a grim future of slavery, starvation and a lingering death. Their master will be the mad and dangerous Lizard King, who holds sway over his land of mutants by the strange powers of black magic and voodoo. Will you risk all in an attempt to save the prisoners?

8. SCORPION SWAMP

presented by
Steve Jackson and Ian Livingstone

All your life you've heard tales of Scorpion Swamp and how it is criss-crossed with treacherous paths leading to the haunts of its disgusting denizens. One step out of place spells a certain and lingering death. You've always been far too wise to venture into that awful marsh, but now it holds out the lure of treasure and glory – and you cannot resist the challenge!

9. CAVERNS OF THE SNOW WITCH

Ian Livingstone

Deep within the Crystal Caves of Icefinger Mountains, the dreaded Snow Witch is plotting to bring on a new ice age. A brave trapper dies in your arms and lays the burden of his mission on your shoulders. But time is running out – will YOU take up the challenge?

10. HOUSE OF HELL

Steve Jackson

Taking refuge in the infamous House of Hell has to be the worst mistake of your life! The dangers of the torrential storm outside are nothing compared to the blood-curdling adventures that await you inside. Who knows how many hapless wanderers like yourself have perished within its gruesome walls? Be warned! Tonight is going to be a night to remember . . .

in preparation

Also by Steve Jackson

FIGHTING FANTASY
The introductory Role-playing game

The world of Fighting Fantasy, peopled by Orcs, dragons, zombies and vampires, has captured the imagination of millions of readers world-wide. Thrilling adventures of sword and sorcery come to life in the Fighting Fantasy Gamebooks, where the reader is the hero, dicing with death and demons in search of villains, treasure or freedom.

Now YOU can create your own Fighting Fantasy adventures and send your friends off on dangerous missions! In this clearly written handbook, there are hints on devising combats, monsters to use, tricks and tactics, as well as two mini-adventures complete with GamesMaster's notes for you to start with. Literally countless adventures await you!

WHAT IS DUNGEONS AND DRAGONS?
John Butterfield, Philip Parker, David Honigmann

A fascinating guide to the greatest of all role-playing games: it includes detailed background notes, hints on play and dungeon design, strategy and tactics, and will prove invaluable for players and beginners alike.